Once Upon A Time
...along my way

Short Stories Based on True Stories

Penny E. Ross

Filidh Publishing

Once Upon A Time...along my way
Short Stories Based on True Stories
Author: Penny E. Ross

Copyright ©2025 by P. E. Ross

ISBN: 978-1-998307-07-4

Published by Filidh Publishing Corp.
Victoria, BC. Canada

Cover Design: Danny Weeds
Cover Photography by P.E. Ross
Interior Photos from the collection of P.E. Ross
Editor: RP Mickelson

Preface

I have loved drawing, doodling, sketching and painting since I was eleven years old. I dreamed of becoming a professional illustrator one day.

In adulthood, many of my friends and relatives encouraged me to keep drawing, which I did with a passionate dedication to mastering my craft. Along the way, I also found a love for photography and writing.

My paintings and photographs have been popular, and I have kept writing short stories since elementary school. Recently, I have been encouraged to move forward with both my art and my writing. I have collaborated with another author by illustrating an expanding series of children's books, and this is my first collection of short stories.

Although my family moved to Vancouver Island when I was a young girl, this book explores the fond memories and wonderment of my early childhood growing up in Southern Saskatchewan.

Dedicated to my loving daughters, Tammy and Sandra.
Thank you for all your assistance with my adventures of writing.

Penny E. Ross
December 15, 2024

4

Growing Up In The Canadian Prairies

Kenneth, Sandra, and Earl

Table of Contents

Fictions and Articles

Chapter 1
Magical Winter Times

I love remembering the magical times I had growing up on the prairies—especially during the winter. Here are a few of my best winter memories:

I wake up and look out the window to see remnants of a blizzard the previous night. Jack Frost left delicate imprints of tiny ice crystals forming a pattern of leaves on the window. They look lacy, as if cut from stencils. I look into the backyard, squinting to see through a small opening in the frost.

Hoar frost clings magically to the window, like crystals on a chandelier—frozen in time. Glittering from reflections of the sun, the ice silently rests on tree branches all over the yard. A soft wind blows snow as it falls gracefully and disappears into the ground. There are huge fluffy mounds of snow, like sculptures forming crests with peaks resting against the fence posts and covering Dad's garden. The remains of the blizzard are still blowing snow, causing it to drift lightly over the spaces Dad is shovelling for our skating rink.

Dad leans against his shovel, looking up with a smile. I don't know how he can be out in this cold temperature every winter and smile. His breath resembles fog escaping from his mouth. It's thirty-five below. Dad says it only takes one day for the ice to freeze at this temperature. That's his forecast, but only if the wind stops blowing.

To prepare the rink, he sprays water from the hose lightly over the whole backyard, covering the garden dirt. Dad then sprays around the wooden clothesline poles and the swings. He sprays until the whole backyard is covered.

"The ice should be good to skate on later today," he says.

"What am I going to do until then?" I reply, "I'm too bored to stay in the house."

My sister Sheryl stays in the house all day reading and doing homework, which could be avoided. She wants to show off to her teacher and get ahead of everyone else. She's smart and always gets As and Bs. Mom and Dad suggest that if I study harder and pay more attention in school, I too could achieve better grades. I tell them I don't have time to study. If I did, I'd never have time to play with my friends, which is very important to me.

The delicious fragrance of mom's irresistible Christmas baking slowly drifts throughout the house. It's a sweet cinnamon aroma coming from apple pies—my favourite dessert. She had already made the Christmas cakes in November. I ask her why she baked the cakes so early.

"The fruits and nuts have to ferment into the cake over time," she replies.

She wraps the cakes in cheesecloth to lock in the flavours and then stores them downstairs in the pantry until the week of Christmas. The nuts and fruit are delicious with a cold glass of milk. Friends and relatives tell Mom her cakes are the best. I can see on Mom's happy face that, for her, it's worth the time she spends on this precious gift she shares at Christmas.

We always give a cake to the generous neighbour who gives us fish from his trips to the nearest lake. It's the same lake my family swims in and where we have picnics on hot summer days on the prairies.

Mom's special traditional Christmas baking is my favourite and leaves me with wonderful memories of my early family life. Mom made mouth-watering Shortbread, Ginger Cookies, Butter Tarts, Matrimonial Date Squares, and Icebox Cookies with red and green cherries on top.

It's a treasure hunt every year for my brothers, who invariably try to find my mom's special places for her Christmas baking. If they do discover the goodies, they never share. They say if they take too many, Mom will notice. I tell them she'll notice no matter how many they take.

Friends and relatives drop by over the holidays for a Christmas toast with Mom and Dad. Every year, there are the same conversations- the weather, future events, social change, and plans for the New Year.

Mom and Dad always celebrate special occasions throughout the year. These include Christmas, Thanksgiving, Easter and birthdays. The traditions are observed over many years to create memories and share life experiences with family members. But the best traditions always come at Christmas, and It's then that my cousins and I sit in front of our tall tree. It's the only time of the year when Mom makes eggnog for all the kids. She serves it cold with whipped cream on top. It's delicious!

The Christmas tree is always covered with sparkling glass ornaments, intricate toys, wooden stars, Gingerbread cookies and strings of popcorn. Sometimes, we add beads from worn-out necklaces that mom doesn't want anymore. The twinkling lights reflect strands of silver tinsel draped over the branches. The smell of pine drifts through the house.

An ornamental angel majestically sits on the top of the tree. Mom tells us every year that the angel is an important reminder that we're celebrating the birth of Jesus in the manger at Bethlehem while angels observe.

My cousins and I share what we wrote in our letters to Santa, hoping they had reached the North Pole in time. That year, I asked for new white figure skates for myself so I wouldn't have to wear hand-me-downs anymore and brown skates for my brothers. I also asked for a pair of pink furry slippers and a pink housecoat.

I wonder out loud why the boys don't wear white skates and why the girls don't wear brown ones.

"I'll never wear white skates," says my oldest brother.

Over the week of Christmas, the dining room table has a white lace tablecloth with bowls of candies, chocolates, jellies, chocolate macaroons, and nuts sitting on it. We crack the nuts with a nutcracker.

My favourite is a beautiful glass bowl full of small oranges that are easy to peel and taste delicious. They're expensive and come in a small wooden box. Dad pries the lid off the box with a hammer, and we see that each of the oranges is wrapped in tissue paper, which makes them even more special. They're called Japanese oranges.

He tells me why the oranges only come to Canada at Christmas time. Apparently, it was customary for Japanese immigrants to Canada in the late nineteenth century to receive packages of oranges to celebrate the Christmas season. They would share these fruits with their neighbours and friends, and this sharing became a Canadian tradition.

Mom keeps the oranges hidden in the master bedroom, the scent drifting through the air. She never scolds anyone if some of the oranges disappear, and sometimes small hands quietly snatch one or two while trying to keep the tissue paper wrapped around them from making a crinkling sound.

I look at my brother Kenneth and say, "Let's go sleigh riding until supper time. The ice will probably be frozen by then."

I hurry into our house and hear Mom say, "Make sure you come home if you're cold and be back in time for dinner! We are having your favourite ...fried chicken."

As Kenneth and I head to the back porch to bundle up into our warmest winter clothes, Dad says, "It's thirty-five below—be careful not to get frostbitten."

I put on my socks and a pair of my dad's woollen socks ... a plastic bread bag over the socks, and pull on black rubber gumboots. I put my toque on, and Mom wraps a long woollen scarf around each of our faces leaving little slits for our mouths and eyes. I put on my mittens and then add another pair of Dad's socks over them.

We head out to a nearby hill, dragging our toboggan. The hill is covered with sleighs and toboggans. Some kids ride down it on cardboard with the shiny side facing the snow. Anything that slides can be used, and the faster, the better! Friends are waving as we all glide down the hill without a care in the world except getting to the bottom and climbing breathlessly back up to repeat the process. I can feel the frost trying to freeze my eyelashes and my nose.

I see a bunch of boys going down the hill sitting on a metal car hood speeding past everyone. Some adults tell their children they shouldn't be on that slope with so many people around because it's too dangerous. After that, most of the children leave, and we don't see them anymore.

I see many of my friends laughing as they fly down the hill without a care in the world while snow hits their faces, leaving them red with cold.

We wipe the snow off the bottom of the toboggan. Kenneth gets in the front, and I start running, pushing the toboggan, then jumping on behind Kenneth, holding him tightly. We laugh and wave to friends climbing back up the hill, hoping for another thrilling ride—faster than the last ones.

The hill has turned from snow into ice in many spots, leaving small ski jumps, lifting our toboggan for a split second, then slamming it down on the snow and ice as it rapidly reaches the bottom.

It feels like it only takes a minute to complete a thrilling ride to the bottom, spinning and dragging our frost-covered mittens along the side of the toboggan to maneuver it. We climb up the slippery slope many times, enjoying the thrill of each descent until it starts to get dark.

We slowly drag our toboggan home. Our faces are very cold, wiping our dripping noses with mittens that are covered in snow. Our fingers and feet are frozen. Ice crystals are clinging to our eyelashes.

Kenneth and I talk and laugh about our first sleigh ride down the hill. We discuss which adventures we'll share with Mom and Dad. We won't mention that we almost fell in front of many other sleds. We go onto the back porch and slowly take off our mittens. Mom helps us pull our numb feet out of stiff rubber boots.
Dad hollers from the kitchen, "The ice is ready when you are."
I look at Kenneth, and we run downstairs to put our skates on.

We change our socks, run out to the skating rink, grab hockey sticks and a puck, and skate onto the backyard rink that has a goalie net my dad made out of wood and plastic for the net. Light shines on the ice with a delicate touch as snowflakes fall onto our faces, touching them lightly.

Kenneth heads into the house after a short time, hungry and cold. I stay out a bit longer and start twirling around the ice, imagining I'm a ballerina with shiny white figure skates. It's been a day of magical winter fun.

***

Penny (author)

Chapter 2
Blackie

My family lived on a farm in southern Saskatchewan. We had a dog named Blackie, who had short hair and big brown eyes. My Dad used to say, "Labs like Blackie have a special double coat that's waterproof."

Blackie didn't bark much, but when strangers came down our driveway, his territorial senses came alive. The would-be guests had to wait in their car until Mom or Dad came out to greet them.

Blackie's favourite activity was chasing sheep with my brother Kenneth and running through the long grass fields to get keep them in order.

Dad would tell us, "Sheep need lots of space, and if they get it, they're easy to care for. They are valuable animals because they eat the grass and provide wool for Mom to make and sell things like warm wool blankets, patchwork quilts and heavy sweaters for the cold winters.

Blackie always tagged along with Kenneth and I. Sometimes, we pretended to be on treasure hunts in the trees and bushes surrounding our home. Mom and Dad reminded us to stop Blackie from barking when he was about to pounce on a deer or raccoon.

We often went down to the river to throw sticks for Blackie to fetch. It didn't matter how far we threw the sticks, he always got them and waited anxiously for us to throw another stick.

Dad understood the psychology of dogs very well and continually lectured us about our dog's nature. "Some dogs don't like water, but Labs do. When Blackie sneezes, it'll sound like honking geese, so don't be alarmed. But if you hear him gagging, he's probably got a small bone lodged in his throat waiting to be coughed up. At times he might look annoyed when woken up suddenly. Always remember, Labs have supersonic hearing."

Every time Mom called us for lunch, we'd turn and run down the hill with Blackie beside us, wagging his tail and flipping his big ears. He always beat us home. At night, he would come to our room to sleep on a soft blanket on the floor in between our beds, but most of the time, he ended up under the blankets at our feet, snoring loudly.

When Kenneth and I played hide and seek on the sandstone rocks near our house, we'd crawl in and out through the holes in the stones while laughing at each other. One day, Blackie made a loud yelping sound, so we ran in his direction.

"Look—he's got porcupine quills stuck in his nose," I exclaimed. "I'm doing to get Dad," said Kenneth breathlessly.

Dad came running back with Kenneth, carrying a pair of pliers from his workshop.

"We're miles and miles away from any veterinarians, and they're too expensive anyway," he said. "I've done this kind of thing before, so let me have a look. These quills can be very painful and should be removed immediately before they become more deeply embedded in the dog's skin."

He then took his pliers and started to talk to the dog quietly as he stroked his back. "If he decides to run, I'll grab him, but if he reacts viciously, we'll have to let him loose for our own safety," noted Dad. "But I don't think he'll run once he knows and trusts us. Talk to him quietly and softly pet him; if he acts agitated, quickly back away."

The quills were like fishhooks with sharp barbs on them. While still talking, Dad grabbed the quills close to Blackie's nose and pulled them out quickly. Blackie lifted his head, yelping, but before he finished, Dad yanked out another one. The dog continued to moan with pain as Dad worked him over. Soon, the ordeal was over, so Dad took out his handkerchief, wiped some blood from our dog's nose, and quietly praised him for being so brave.

Kenneth and I looked at each other with tears in our eyes, feeling Blackie's pain. Dad gently lifted him up and carried him into the house. Mom covered him with a warm blanket and rubbed some healing salve on his wounds. Kenneth and I sat beside him, talking softly until he finally fell asleep.

"I don't think he'll get close to porcupines anymore," said Dad.

We enjoyed many more days with Blackie running and playing. He met us at the school bus stop every day. While we were at home, he was our constant companion. But one day, he didn't come to the bus stand to meet us and wasn't home when we got there.

"He was here all day and will probably get back soon," said Mom. "Maybe he's out chasing rabbits."

We called him and looked everywhere, but he was not to be found. I lay awake all night worrying about our dog. Maybe he got more porcupine quills in his nose, and no one was there to help him, I thought.

We never saw Blackie again.

Years later, when we were adults, Mom and Dad told us that our uncle shot and killed Blackie because he would not stop chasing his sheep and occasionally injuring them. That made me feel very angry.

"I worried about Blackie for years—how could you let your uncle kill him?" I stated angrily.

"Penny, that's the way farmers live. If animals become a nuisance, they get rid of them," replied Dad.

"That's why I never became a farmer," I responded.

***

Sheryl, Penny, and Kenneth. Beloved dog, Blackie

Chapter 3
Fishing with Dad on the Boundary Dam

Sometimes, we would take a break from farm work. Dad loved to fish, and he took us with him to ice fish in the winter and troll in his boat on the local lakes in the summer. I'll never forget fishing with my dad.

One Saturday, Dad was taking me and my brother Kenneth ice fishing. The aromas of bacon and scones were wafting through the house. *Dad's already getting his gear ready so I better hurry*, I thought. As we rushed to the breakfast table, Mom said, "Sit down and eat; your dad will wait."

We each gobbled down bacon and eggs, a cheese scone and a glass of milk. Then I jumped up from the table, hurried to the back door and put on my winter coat, boots, scarves, and mittens. Dad was already heading out the door. I ran down the outside stairs to get my worn-out skates, hockey stick, fishing rod and tackle box. I got that box for my birthday when I was five, and by then, I'd had it for seven years. *Wow—it's lasted a long time*, I noted.

Blackie, our dog, came running out and jumped into the red truck we have had forever. It was Ken's turn to sit in the front seat with Dad, so I jumped into the back seat with the dog. Ken turned Dad's regular country music stations to rock and roll. This would initiate a continual debate all the way to the lake. Dad would say, "How can you listen to that racket?"

The Boundary Dam was approximately twenty miles away on a slippery back road. Dad always mentioned, "If we slip on black ice, we could end up in a ditch."

One time, we stopped to help a man pull his truck out of a ditch. Of course, Dad told him, "Slow down, or next time, you might end up in a more serious situation." The guy thanked Dad, and they shook hands. Then we got back to our trip.

I watched the snowflakes softly spiral down, hitting the truck windows and forming different patterns before they melted. Some of the flakes never did melt. Instead, they formed beautiful frost patterns on the windows.

Dad's truck doesn't have a good heater, and we got cold before we reached the ice to fish.

That day, we finally did arrive at the dam after a long, dragged-out drive because Dad stopped to help a lady on the side of the road with her flat tire. She was so grateful that she offered to pay Dad, but he refused to take any money. Once we got there, we could drive on the ice to the hut Dad and Kenneth had built. It was made with scraps of material that had accumulated in our backyard.

Dad said, "We'll start by building skids to put the hut on, and then pull it over the ice to where the fish are. In the spring, we'll push it back to shore."

Dad unlocked the door of the hut, and we rushed in to escape the frozen wind that was taking our breath away! The hut had a small wooden stove sitting on a shelf in the corner to keep us warm and cozy. There was a small window on one side and long benches on two walls. Dad brought orange and green cushions from his boat to cover the benches. Mom knitted orange blankets to cover the benches and us. There were shelves to store matches, candles, fishing equipment, scarves, mittens and gloves and a flashlight. Then he drilled a hole right in the middle of the hut and hammered a circle of thin ice off the top. We were now ready to fish!

I placed my Lone Ranger lunch kit beside Kenneth's Yogi Bear one. They were both filled with delicious lunches of sandwiches, desserts and a thermos of hot chocolate. Ken and I sat on the bench to put our skates on.

I hurriedly unlatched the door, stepped out and felt Jack Frost nipping my nose through the slits of my warm woollen scarf. I could see my friends, Tom, Kevin and Brenda, skating with their metal blades gliding over the bumpy ice. Ripples and dips were apparent in that ice, which created frozen wispy waves against the shores. It reminded me of the windy lakes in summer with the heavy winds that were blowing.

We made goalposts with small chunks of ice and divided into teams. Kevin slammed the puck into the goal, giving their team a head start. We played until we couldn't feel our fingers anymore.

"Let's break for lunch," hollered Brenda, as her voice was carried away by the wind.

Ken and I could feel the warmth coming from the stove as we went back into the hut. Dad was having a lucky fishing day so I knew we would have fish and chips for supper. I found a spot on the bench that felt warm and removed the lid of my thermos so I could sip the hot chocolate inside, throwing one of Mom's knitted blankets on. Then, I removed the wax paper from a bologna and mustard sandwich and a lemon square. Mom made great lunches!

Dad began to light some candles to bring more light into the hut. "Go have another game," said Dad. "I'll let you know when I'm ready to leave."

We skated for another hour before Dad stepped out of the hut with his gear under both arms, heading for the car. He opened the trunk and pulled out two ropes, which he tied around the bumper and handed each of us an end.

"Hold on tight," he bellowed.

As the vehicle started moving, the rope tightened, and we started to move forward with our skates maneuvering to keep us balanced. Soon, we were moving very fast, steering in and out until the car came to a slow stop.

"Dad, thanks for doing that," I said when we got back into the car. "It's the best fun I've ever had in my whole life."

We went fishing with Dad as far back as I can remember. Those experiences will always be great memories for Kenneth and me. I plan to keep ice fishing in the winter and trout fishing in the summer for the rest of my life. For some reason, we never did tell Mom of the ride on the ice.

***

Sandra, Penny, Kenneth, Earl, Judy and Dad

Chapter 4
Turkey Time

Every year, our extended family takes turns cooking at New Year's, Easter, Thanksgiving, and Christmas. There are usually anywhere from twenty-five to forty family members present.

Mom's dinners, of course, were the best. She is a great cook and taught my three sisters and me how to prepare a delicious meal.

She loves cooking so much that she did it for a job. Mom used to work at a nursing home cooking for up to eighty seniors. Sometimes, I'd help her at that nursing home if I didn't have other plans. There were always huge metal pots of potatoes and vegetables boiling on the stove and at least four large turkeys roasting in the oven. She'd also prepare lots of mouthwatering pies, fresh breads and a variety of salads. Just before the scrumptious dinners were served, Mom made gravy. And she had strict rules about mealtimes even at home—insisting, for example, that we all ate while the food was hot.

Thinking back over the years, I can't remember my mom ever complaining about how physically difficult her job was lifting those heavy pots, frozen turkeys and bowls full of food. She started working when I was fourteen. Her shift then was from one to six pm five days a week, and she'd do all the prep work for our own supper before she left for work. My older sister was never available, so I'd come home right after school to babysit my four siblings and cook the food Mom had prepared for supper. I was lucky because my dad wasn't fussy. He'd eat burnt or over-boiled meals and never complain.

While I was helping at the nursing home and cooking for my dad and siblings, I learnt to enjoy cooking. When I was older, I was the one who cooked for all my relatives. It wasn't hard—finding enough chairs was often the biggest task. We used kitchen and dining room chairs.

We had so many guests my sister sometimes asked,
"Why don't we use lawn chairs?"

"This'll give my sisters something to gossip about." I was shocked whenever she talked like that—but she rarely did. My memories of those get-togethers are precious

Adults sat at the main table, and children sat beside it, not far away. It always worked out and added fun to the occasion, Mom used to say.

One year, we were going to Aunt Dorothy's and Uncle Merle's house. I've had lots of relatives that I didn't see very often. For example, there were twelve children in my cousin Marilynn's family. Nancy, my cousin, meets us at the door and directs us to the bedroom to put our coats on the bed. I can hear the laughter in the living room. Some of the relatives have few chances to gather every year. They're always busy with other tasks, jobs, farming chores or travel. Aunt Dorothy was busy in the kitchen with Mom giving her a hand cutting up vegetables for the salad. I heard her ask Mom if she wouldn't mind making the gravy.

Mom replies, "Of course I will. Why don't you watch me? That way, you'll learn how to make it yourself."

That never happened. Ever since I was a child, my mom was a master at making gravy and luckily, she taught me her secrets! Once, when I lived beside a young couple, we eventually made friends. They were having a dinner party, and she'd overheard my husband bragging about my cooking.

"Would you mind making the gravy, Penny?" she asked. "I'm no good at making it. I've tried many times, but it just won't work for me. It either tastes like water or forms greasy lumps that taste like flour."

So, while they entertained their company, I snuck in the back door, made the gravy and tiptoed out. When I told Mom, she laughed.

After mom made the gravy, she and Aunt Dorothy had a minute to visit with the guests before the turkey and stuffing were placed into the oven. Later, I was sitting beside Aunt Dorothy. She heard the stove buzzer go off, reminding us that the turkey needed to be checked.

She looked at me and asked, "I don't want to bother your mom. Do you think you could give me a hand with the turkey?"

I nodded my head and answered, "Sure, that'll be no problem."

It was always exciting to be asked to help in the kitchen because it was usually off-bound for me until it was time to do the dishes, clean the counters, or sweep the floor.

"Here, take these potatoes off the stove," said Aunt Dorothy as she handed me a pair of pink potholders with bright white daisies. "I'm going to bring the roaster out and place it on that white platter beside the cupboard."

The oven was hot, and its smothering heat reminded me to be careful. I turned my face away as I bent over ready to help. She then slowly started to pull the roaster out of the oven and looked over at me.

"Grab the handle and lift," she shouted. Just as she spoke, the oven rack slanted forward, and that's when the disaster happened. When the lid was removed from the roaster so Dorothy could check it, the turkey pot shifted forward because the oven rack was slanting. Aunt Dorothy tried to balance the hot oven rack, avoid getting her arms burnt, and slide the roaster back into the oven, but it was too late! The delicious brown turkey slipped out of the roaster and flew across the kitchen floor as it spun around with its golden drumsticks swirling tightly against the bird's body. Luckily, all the stuffing never escaped before the turkey hit the wall. I looked at Aunt Dorothy. Her face was red from the heat of the oven. In a weak and high-pitched voice, she gasped, "Oh my goodness!"

I thought Aunt Dorothy might actually start crying. Thinking quickly, she threw a tea towel over the turkey and picked it up with the potholders still in her hands. She moved quickly to the kitchen sink and put the hot bird under the tap to wash it off—holding it upright so the water wouldn't ruin the stuffing. I stood by in horror, not sure what to do. I was feeling guilty because I was laughing under my breath. It was hilarious for me to see the turkey fly out of the roaster. Dorothy quickly put the turkey into the pan, looked at me and whispered, "Shh." I quietly nodded my head. We put the turkey on the platter, and my aunt put the stuffing in a large glass bowl. Just then, Mom entered the kitchen, completely unaware of the earlier catastrophe.

We all sat down to dinner, and my uncle said grace. Then he cut the turkey and laid all the white and brown slices on a large plate, dark meat on the right, white on the left. No one was the wiser that the turkey had tragically flown across the kitchen just twenty minutes before. Aunt Dorothy acted like normal, as if nothing had happened. The meal was delicious and had all the trimmings. After supper, Dad and my uncles plopped themselves into living room chairs.

Dad said, "I should never have eaten so much. I couldn't eat another bite." Everyone else nodded in agreement.

My aunts were in the kitchen filling trays with mouthwatering desserts like fruit cake, butter tarts, cookies, pecan pie, and my favourite, apple crisp. The smell of fresh coffee was wafting through the kitchen as all our family members chatted about the events of the year. I sat across the table from Aunt Dorothy, knowing we had a secret. She looked at me during supper and winked with a grin on her face. Nobody else knew about the turkey event. It was our little secret forever. I'd ever had the best turkey dinner.

When I got older, we decided to tell Mom. At first, she gasped and then burst out laughing.

***

Sheryl, Penny, and Nancy

Chapter 5
The Blizzard and the Baby

"There's going to be a blizzard today," Mom told us one day in the winter of 1956.

The wind was slowly forming snowdrifts on the road, blowing them up against our house and fences.

"The weatherman said it's going to be one to remember and advised us not to drive on any roads right now," Dad added.

The next day, Mom called us to come inside for supper as we frolicked in the snow with the temperature of thirty degrees below zero.

"You can go out after supper and build an igloo," she said.
I walked up to the front door, hearing the soft crunching of snow under my feet. They felt cold like they might be frostbitten. I could hear children shouting with glee as the snow flurries increased.

Mom always had interesting ways to describe the snow: a crystal carpet, a quilt of nature or a cloud with a silver lining. Every winter, she would think of another descriptive metaphor. Just two days before the weather turned, snow hanging from our gutters turned into icicles. Mom said they looked like frozen daggers; and don't walk under the eaves.

The prairie snow was perfect for building igloos. We would just sprinkle it with a tiny bit of moisture so the snow would harden. If conditions were right, we could produce enough cut ice blocks to erect a large igloo that would actually hold together.

My sister Sheryl and I helped our younger siblings, Sandra and Earl, build a snowman that afternoon to keep them busy and out of our way while we built an igloo.

Later, I was hungry after skating and tobogganing all day with my friends. Mom usually made a delicious stew on Saturdays with scrumptious biscuits and fresh vegetables from the garden that had been stored in the cooler in the basement.

My hands were often still red from the cold even after I'd finished my supper. Mom would tell us to hold them under warm water to relieve the pain.

"You're old enough to know when your skin is getting frost burnt," she lectured us repeatedly.

Blackie used to snuggle close to the fireplace in the living room, waiting for his supper, which was always composed of our leftovers. By then, he was usually tired from running up and down the snow hills all day. I used to put him behind me on a toboggan, and he'd hold on with his back feet on my shoulders and his shiny black ears flopping up and down as we flew down a hill without a care in the world.

In those days in southern Saskatchewan, the winters were very cold, and the summers were dry and hot. I always thought it was interesting how we could freeze in the winter and have such hot summer days.

On hot summer afternoons, Mom made us stay in the house for hours until it cooled down. Mom's famous last words as we finally could leave the house: "Please be careful, and don't step on any rusty nails."

My friends didn't live too far away. We did whatever was dangerous so we could have real adventures. We never did get our raft made that we dreamt of floating down the river on.

In 1958, Kenneth became jealous of one of his friends.
"Edwin's going to Disney Land with his family for the Christmas holidays. He's so lucky!"

Mom and Dad always told us one year we would go to Disney Land, but that year never came.

"There's nobody to take care of all our animals," Dad would say. "And with a new calf coming every spring, we've got to make sure it gets the right diet so it'll survive and get fat before we take it to the butcher's. There are also chickens, ducks and turkeys to consider," he'd say, "They have to be killed and frozen so we can have food all winter."

The truth was clear: even a small farm like ours took a lot of work year-round. There was never going to be a time for vacations.
We all had fresh milk from our cow, Bossy, at every meal. In the spring of 1958, Bossy was ready to have a baby. Our kittens swarmed around, waiting for a squirt of warm milk to come their way.

Mom told me, "A cow's pregnant for nine months and you have to stop milking it after seven months. That's eight weeks before the calf is born." The calf is small and cute and learns to stand right away, stumbling and trying hard to get up.

A blizzard was getting louder and louder as we ate our supper. I could see white snow blowing back and forth, by icy cold winds coming from the north. Then, the phone on our kitchen wall rang, and Dad answered it.

He hung up the phone and got ready to head into town because it was his night to be on emergency duty. Dad was a mechanic and worked hard all day. He had six children, and we ate a lot—especially my brothers Kenneth and Earl.

Dad never complained when it was his turn for emergency towing and that occurred many times over the cold winter nights on the prairies. People just slipped on the ice or slid off the road. Some cars just wouldn't start because people hadn't plugged their cars in overnight to keep the battery and other parts of the car from freezing. My sister Sheryl often went with Dad on emergency runs to keep him company. On those times, Blackie was always the co-pilot.

However, on this particularly cold night, Dad told me it was my turn to come with him, so I rushed to my room and put on two sweaters, two pairs of socks, my heavy-duty mitts, my toque and wool scarf. Blackie was waiting impatiently by the door, panting with his long pink tongue hanging out and drooling foam onto the kitchen floor.

Dad jumped into his truck and warmed it up while waiting for us. Blackie and I jumped into the back seat. It was only a mile from our garage. Dad unlocked the garage door and grabbed his keys and walkie-talkie. Just then, his boss told him a car had gone off the road. Inside, there was a man who'd been driving his wife to the hospital to deliver a baby. Blackie and I jumped onto the front seat. The wind was blowing hard—forming snow banks across the roads. Visibility was terrible; the roads were icy and covered in snow.

For me, this was a very exciting event. We were going to help make sure a pregnant woman got to the hospital. The blizzard and poor vision had caused the car to go into a ditch. Dad was heading fast to the given location. When we arrived, a man was doing his best to shovel his automobile out .

He looked very stressed and turned to Dad in a panic.
"My wife's in labour," he cried—"Please help us because I don't know what to do."

Dad calmly hooked a chain to the fender of the partially buried car and began to pull it out of the ditch with his tow truck. He could see a woman lying in the back seat, wrapped in blankets. Blackie and I were sitting in the truck, watching all the excitement. The trapped car slowly started to climb out of the steep crevice with its wheels spinning wildly as snow was being thrown all over the road.

Dad opened his truck's door and went over to the man. I could see the poor fellow shaking his head. Dad walked back towards Blackie and me in the truck.

"The car is really buried," Dad told me. "We'll have to drive this man and his wife to the hospital. She's in bad pain and needs to get there as soon as possible."

Dad helped the man carry his wife into the warm tow truck. Blackie jumped to the floor, and I moved over. We headed out after Dad talked to the boss on his walkie-talkie and let him know what was happening.

All of a sudden, the woman started screaming out, "It hurts!"

Her husband answered, "Hold on darling, we'll be there in twenty minutes. Then she started to cry even louder.

"My water just broke," she moaned in dismay.

"What does that mean?" I asked my dad.

"The baby is ready to be born," he responded.

"There's a side road up ahead," said the man, "Can you pull in there out of the way of traffic?"

"Yes, I can," Dad said.

"Why are we stopping, Dad?" I asked.

"Don't talk right now, Penny. Just make as much room as you can for the woman so she can lie on the back seat."

Blackie and I moved over as close to the door as we could. We could see the man putting his wife on her back and covering her up with his jacket. I couldn't believe the shocked look on my dad's face because the woman was tossing and screaming as her husband held her hand. My dad went outside and covered her legs with a blanket because they were sticking out into the cold air.
She kept crying, moaning, and finally screamed,
"It's coming!"
I looked at Dad in bewilderment, but he was busy trying to help the man do something. All of a sudden, I heard a crying sound. Then I saw the man hold up a baby and give it to his wife wrapped in his jacket. It was a boy, and he had blood on his face and neck! She smiled and took the baby.

"What a night," Dad laughed, and the man laughed back.

"Congratulations," said Dad.

Sometime later, a truck stopped along the road in front of our tow truck. A man got out carrying a lantern. He looked at Dad, the woman and the man and realized what had just occurred.

"Wow, this was quite a tow job," said Dad. "But I'm not going to charge you anything for it. Now I'll run you up to the hospital."

Dad and I travelled home in silence. After a while, he nudged me and said, "I can't believe you don't have any questions."

I turned and took my dad's arm and hugged it. "That was very exciting, Dad, and I'll never forget it. Those people were so lucky that you were on duty tonight. You were so kind and helpful."

We had a great story to tell my mom when we got home.
"Slow down," she said, "Do you mean to tell me that a baby was just born in dad's truck?

I shook my head and walked away. I can still hear Mom and Dad laughing.

About five days later, the man, woman and baby boy came to visit us. They wanted to thank my dad. The man called Dad's boss to tell him that a wonderful thing had happened when his wife gave birth.

"How many kids does Mr. Ross have?" He asked Dad's employer.

"Mr. Hutchinson—he has six—four girls and two boys."

Mr. Hutchinson knocked on the door one night. While we were having coffee and cookies, Mr. Hutchinson went out to his car and came back in with six brown bags of candy.

What a day to remember! My times with Dad on the emergency calls were simply the best, and I'll never forget them.

***

Chapter 6
As the Seasons Turned

My family lived on farms at two different times when I was growing up. My father was a mechanic and worked in town when he wasn't busy doing farm work. Mom was a city girl and would never adjust to life on the farm.

I enjoyed all my adventures growing up on those farms and wanted to live on a farm when I grew up. Dad talked a lot about how farm work was never finished. There were always tasks or chores that would have to be completed before one day ended and another started.

Dad was always up early, even before Rocky the rooster crowed. He'd first check on all the animals. Cows and pigs went to the butcher in early spring. There were also chickens and turkeys to deal with. And rats—who were always checking out the grains we fed our cows.

I still wonder why Dad always liked country life. He got home from work, ate supper, and then went out to check on all the farm work left to do. It seemed like he was always working. He went to bed late and got up before sunrise—never complaining. He always told me being in the country was peaceful and beautiful.

"Just listen to the sounds of the birds, crickets and frogs," he used to say. "The constant noise of traffic and sirens in the city are gone. Just breathe in that clean air and appreciate the beauty of your surroundings." He also told me growing your own food required dedication, resilience, and willingness to adapt to the challenges of rural living.

Mom said, "I always enjoy seeing the results of your dad's hard work. I certainly appreciate what he does."

My brother Kenneth and I helped Dad around the farm. There was always something to do. We had to milk the cows twice a day, feed the chickens and cows, repair the fences, and paint the barn. Every day, Dad would come up with a new list of chores, and they never ended. While the younger girls helped Mom in the house, I preferred to be outside doing stuff for Dad.

One day, I asked him, "Why are barns always painted red?"

"Because in the early days, farmers painted their barns with a protective coating of linseed oil to keep the wood from weathering. They often mixed the oil with animal fat, which prevented the growth of mould and fungi and gave the paint a red-orange colour."

As the years went by, I found farming could be physically demanding and require long hours. Dad always found satisfaction from working on the farm and being outside in the fresh air. There were hot days in the summer and freezing cold winters in southern Saskatchewan.

Mom kept busy in the house all day. She was frightened of all the animals—except for chickens. She enjoyed taking care of the garden and worked for hours every day on it. Watering wasn't an easy chore because we had to carry big buckets from the well.

My brothers made many trips carrying water back and forth, and Mom appreciated it. The garden was beautiful, covered in wildflowers between rows and rows of vegetables. You could see the paths we made through the tall grass as we walked back and forth from the well.

Dad had a few fruit trees and bushes that he covered with gunnysacks to keep from freezing over the winter. We'd use the gunny sacks to carry potatoes if we were going to the neighbours' to trade cheese and other food items for the potatoes. Dad would plant a whole acre of potatoes. When we lived in town, Dad planted potatoes in our front yard. My friends would make fun of it, and Dad would laugh when I told him. When all the vegetables and fruits were ready to pick, we all participated whether we liked to or not. Earl and Sandra helped Dad pick vegetables, putting them in wicker baskets at the end of each row.

Dad built a tall wooden box with a door which he kept in the basement to store potatoes, turnips, and carrots for the winter. We'd then dig them up after all the other fruits and vegetables were eaten.

Sheryl and I helped Mom with the canning. We'd clean the vegetables and fruits and place them in sterilized jars, setting them carefully on a rack and lowering them into a pot of boiling water before sealing the lids tightly. Boiling them removed the oxygen remaining in the jars, which helped to form a tight seal and kept any bacteria out of the food. We kept the jars on tea towels in the cupboards all night long while we listened to the lids pop.

Mom made dozens of piecrusts to fill with blueberries and raspberries and keep in the freezer for tasty desserts over the winter. We ate canned preserves throughout the winter, which included peas, beans and tomatoes. My parents had six children to feed on a limited budget, so the canning really helped. Mom's dill pickles with garlic were the best. One year, she won first place for them at the country fair. She put the ribbon on the wall in the kitchen.

We milked the cows, churned butter and cream and made delicious fudge with the cream. We bought sugar, flour, salt and yeast in a nearby town. Even though my mom wasn't crazy about country living, she did enjoy the preserving process.

Once a month, we'd dress up in our church clothes to get ready to go to town. Mom would give us ten cents to buy whatever we wanted, and I inevitably headed for Samson's Candy Store. Several elderly men would gather outside the store, smoking cigars, discussing the weather, telling stories and reminiscing about the old days. Nevertheless, we were so tired after church that we always fell asleep on the way home.

April was the month to get baby chicks. Dad would usually buy some from one of our neighbours and bring them home in a cardboard box that had little holes in its sides so the birds could breathe. One year, he brought the chicks into our house and put them on the oven door to keep them warm until they grew larger. He lifted the lid on the box to show us, and I was astonished. They were pink and blue mixed with shades of yellow. They stayed in those boxes for two weeks, and we could hear them peeping all day long during that time. When I held them, they felt like tiny balls of fluff pecking away at my fingers. I never wanted to think we'd be eating them one day. But over time, they did grow, and eventually, Kenneth helped Dad prepare chicken soup out of them.

As soon as the chicks started growing, we moved them into the chicken coup. Dad had installed a light bulb to provide them with some heat to help them make the transition into adulthood. He built feeder pans and troughs so the chickens could eat and drink without having to go into their fenced yard. It was my responsibility to keep the water fountains filled every day with fresh water. The chick nursery was safe because the wire fence kept the cats, skunks, rats and foxes out.

We burned wood in the stove all day during the winter to keep the house warm. It was still chilly under the quilts that Grandma had made all summer for us. Mom used to heat water on the stove to fill our large silver metal bathtub that sat beside the wood stove. When the water pump in the kitchen wouldn't pump water, we'd carry water from the well. My sister and brothers would bathe first, and Dad went last. This was hard to adjust to since we always wanted hot water, so we had to change it often.

On Sundays after church, our whole community would have picnics at the river. It was fun swimming, playing baseball, catching grasshoppers and chasing chickens. But my favourite month was December.

During that month, my mom would be busy baking for the church Christmas concert. After the concert, everyone attended a potluck celebration in the Community Hall. Mom would always bring a red velvet cake with creamy icing in the middle and on top. The icing would slither generously down the sides of the cake, making my mouth water. In the middle of the cake, she'd put Christmas decorations, usually holly with red berries.
There was a huge Christmas tree in the middle of the floor at the Community Hall. The lights on that tree blinked on and off, lighting up the tinsel. And there was always a white angel ornament on the very top.

Earl, Sandra, and Judy would always sing in the Christmas Concert, which meant they had to practice for months at school. As the day grew closer, they'd get more and more excited. The entire main street would be lined with cars and trucks from our village. It was standing room only inside the Hall because no one wanted to miss the concert. The children were always excited as they waited for their turns on stage. They knew the concert was over when the piano started to play "Here Comes Santa Claus," and Santa hurried through the main door with a small gift for every child.

We spent five winters on the farm and then moved back to the city. When I look back over the years, I remember with fondness all the adventures I shared with my family during our years on the farm. Living on a farm caused us to make many adjustments, but after a while, I didn't even think about the differences between farm life and the city. However, as I got older, I realized that I'd learned many important life lessons from living on a farm.

***

Mom and Dad tying the tarp down on our way to the lake.

Chapter 7
Picnic Time

Mom always cooked chicken for our annual family picnic at the lake and placed it in a worn-out wicker basket. It was at those gatherings that I interacted with all my cousins.

We all noticed that her wicker basket was worn and asked why she was still using it; she'd say, "Your dad and I used this basket when we were dating, and my grandmother and grandfather had it before us."

I asked her, "But why don't we get you a new picnic basket?" She used to ignore me when I asked that question and just kept on preparing another picnic in the old, tattered basket. She'd wrap the chicken in foil to keep it warm and put the potato salad into a separate container to keep it cool. She'd make a large pitcher of grape juice and put ice cubes in it, leaving the jug in our fridge until it was time to leave. She also often made a delicious ambrosia salad full of pineapples, cherries and mandarin oranges. Then there were always wieners and hot dog buns packed in plastic bags.

On my fourteenth birthday, on August 18th, 1962, we celebrated the milestones at our annual picnic.

"Penny, please wrap the plastic forks, knives and spoons in paper napkins," Mom told me. My parents did the same thing every year. And it happened the same way that year. Dad picked up the heavy wicker basket and put it in the trunk of his car.

Mom reminded us," Don't forget your swimsuits." I grabbed Sandra, Earl and Judy's bathing suits because they were taking too long to find them. Kenneth, Sheryl and I already had ours ready, along with our beach towels. Kenneth muttered something under his breath as he grabbed the baseball bat, balls and gloves.

"Why do I always have to find them?" I asked.

Sheryl was helping mom fill Judy's diaper bag. Once Dad had the trunk packed, he looked at the list of everything we should have packed for the lake.

"Looks like we are all prepared for the big day," he said. "If we've forgotten anything, we'll go without or improvise. Mom's good at improvising."

"Everybody get in the car now," Dad said with a commanding tone.

Mom was still in the house rushing around, going over her own checklist.

Judy sat between Mom and Dad in the front seat. Sheryl, Kenneth, Sandra, Earl, and I jumped into the back seat. Earl crawled up onto the back window, holding his plastic pail and shovel.

Earl was born with clubfeet and wore braces on his legs for a while. He was in the hospital for the first year of his life. Doctors operated on his feet. At night, he wore shoes with a steel bar hooked to the inside of each shoe. Mom explained to us,
"The brace helps keep Earl's hips in place when he's not in the hospital having operations."

I didn't really understand how that helped fix his feet until I grew up. Whenever Mom was sad, I knew the next day Dad would drive her to Regina so she could spend the day with Earl as he lay in a hospital bed. I went to Regina with them in the summer of that year. Mom held Earl for most of the time, caring for him and feeding him. For most of the ride home, I could hear Mom quietly crying. But Dad tried to comfort her by saying, "We'll come back next week on my day off."

Many years later, I found out that the same operation that kept Earl in the hospital for almost a year now takes ninety minutes. Parents can bring their children home the same day as the surgery after the patient is fitted with a cast.

As we headed to the picnic that year, Sheryl was organizing a stack of books sitting on her lap. She didn't swim very often and preferred to sit in the shade reading. It seemed like all she ever did was read and watch game shows on TV.

I told Mom, "I don't like game shows."

Mom replied, "It's because you'll have to sit still for twenty minutes!"

At that, I shrugged my shoulders and thought, what's wrong with climbing trees, burning ant hills and swimming in the swamp? Sheryl used to constantly talk on our telephone until Mom and Dad would tell her, "It's time to hang up."

We couldn't talk on the phone at dinnertime. If any friends came to the door while we were eating dinner, they'd have to wait outside until we were finished eating and doing the dishes.

During the summers, Dad would drive down gravel roads just for the fun of it. Inevitably, his car would go up and down over the clouds of dust that sprayed the air and made it difficult for us to see out the windows.

But once autumn arrived, the large maple trees growing along the road swayed gracefully, and the wind rustled through their leaves which would soon be gone.

During the winter months, it was freezing cold in southern Saskatchewan—until at least April. Every spring, Mom would say, "The tulips are poking out of the ground, so spring's just around the corner."

In those days, we didn't have air conditioning in our cars, so when the weather got hot, we suffered. And we could only keep the windows open for a short while because of the dust. Driving to the lake was torture because all the kids were squished into the back seat.

On that particular day, Kenneth didn't say much, and Sheryl was busy reading until she got car sick. "Sandra's being a good girl playing quietly with her dolls," noted Mom.

When we finally arrived, there were many people having their last picnics of the year with friends and family. Dad stopped the car. "Don't go anywhere until this car's unpacked," he said.

We didn't ask questions when his voice sounded gruff. When I finished helping my dad, I asked, "Can I go swimming now?"

Dad nodded his head and said, "Have fun and don't do silly things in the water! It's your birthday, so have fun!"

Mom reminded me to keep an eye on Kenneth because he was younger than me and couldn't swim. She was busy putting Judy in the carriage with a screen to cover it so the bugs wouldn't bite her. There were many mosquitoes at the lake that summer and Mom always carried a bottle of calamine lotion to help reduce the itching caused by their bites. Listening to the laughter from my cousins, who were already swimming, I was anxious to join them.

Most of my cousins lived on farms and needed to stay around the farm in the cold winters to care for all their animals. They liked to take a short break just before thrashing time. In those days, farmers planted their crops in the early spring as soon as they were able to get their tractors and machines onto the wet, muddy fields. The weather was always a big factor for them. They waited anxiously to plant their fields once the snow melted. Some even prayed for rain and sun. So, when all of this was completed, they could take a few days off to relax.

Once mom finished helping Sandra, Earl and Judy into their swimsuits, she wandered over with her lawn chair in one arm and Judy in the other, looking for a shady spot to catch up with the latest happenings in her sisters' lives. Dad walked over to the horseshoe pits, where the men were playing until they called for lunch.

I slowly took one step into the lake. It was freezing cold! Kenneth started splashing water all over me, so I splashed him back. After a while, the water didn't feel as cold anymore. Everybody was now jumping off the wharf and then climbing back up to jump again. After hours of splashing, doing cannonballs and hitting a beach ball, I felt hungry. By then, my mom and aunts were busy preparing lunch.

I looked towards the picnic table covered with mom's red and white checkered tablecloth. The excitement didn't stop my appetite. Mom smiled and said, "Lunch is ready; go dry yourselves off."

Grabbing my towel, I headed for the table adorned with scrumptious food. Mom's fried chicken was first on my plate then came two scoops of potato salad and a fresh white bun. I poured a glass of Welch's grape soda and headed for the shade. Gobbling down my food and feeling full, I made a return trip to a table covered with desserts. A cake smothered in chocolate icing with plump strawberries on top was sitting in plain sight, and some large cookies with chocolate chips clinging to their sides were right next to it. My grandma had also created her special jelly rolls filled with peaches and whipped cream. I knew I'd have to return to the tables once my stomach settled. I spotted a plate of devilled eggs and decided to have one before they all disappeared. I always wondered why swimming made me so hungry because baseball and soccer never did! I ate so much food when swimming that I felt like exploding.

Mom commented,"You can't go swimming for an hour after eating."

What a stupid rule, I thought. Slipping my jeans on over my bathing suit, I ran to catch up with my dad and uncles as they headed for the baseball field. Kenneth grabbed the bats, balls and gloves out of Dad's trunk and trailed behind us. Sheryl never liked playing baseball, and Sandra was too young to keep track of foul balls. Our team's name was Hard to Catch. Earl couldn't play because of his braces.

I'd occasionally dream that bullies would appear and take Earl away to a moat where they'd tease him by threatening to throw him in the water. But as soon as Earl got rid of his braces, that dream disappeared. I never told my parents about it because they didn't need another worry. Earl is now sixty years old and takes part in any sport he wants.

"Batter up," my uncle hollered. Dad slammed the ball out to the fence, and I took off from second base, running as fast as I could to home plate with Dad close behind. Kenneth was a great pitcher and got the next two players out. We won the game by one hit. After it was over, I was tired, just like the rest of the team.

I threw my jeans on the ground and raced Sandra to the water for another swim as it was getting dark. I swam for another hour and changed into dry clothes for the wiener roast. Dad was sharpening tree branches to roast the wieners. Logs were quickly burning, and their embers glowed brightly as new pieces of wood continually replaced them.

I sat down in a circle of relatives and friends. Kenneth and Dad, along with others, were strumming their guitars and banjos, bringing back memories of earlier picnics. As always, Mom had a good supply of blankets for us to cover us so we could avoid the smoky air flow coming from the fire. After roasting wieners and hot, sticky marshmallows, I got burned. A piece of burning marshmallow fell on my leg, leaving a scar that's still there. By this time, some of us were so tired we started to fall asleep leaning against a bench. Judy was starting to fuss and wanted her own bed.

In the morning, we helped Dad pack the car, said our goodbyes to those we wouldn't see until next year and got into the vehicle. Dad called out to those staying behind, "I hope your crops thrive this year."

Earl was asleep in the back window, hugging his stuffed teddy bear. Sandra and Kenneth were leaning on Sheryl and me.

Sheryl grinned and said, "I finished one of my books that I needed to read for the summer."

"Not as much fun as I had today," I replied.

When we got home, I went to bed, glad to be snuggling under warm covers. We all had so much fun today, I thought. It was the best birthday celebration ever!

I fell asleep and dreamed that we lived at the lake permanently, swam every day and had wiener roasts every night. It was a wonderful dream.

***

Family picnic at the lake.

Chapter 8
Aunt Nellie

Aunt Nellie and her brother Fred lived on a farm not far from our house. One day, she invited us over for dinner. Mom baked a lemon loaf with vanilla cream icing to surprise her and Uncle Fred. Aunt Nellie always welcomed us warmly. She said she liked our visits because it gave her a chance to cook a meal. Her favourite pastime was baking. She'd take some of her baked goods to the baker in her small wicker basket. Her sugar cookies were always a big seller there.

When we arrived for dinner, I got out and unchained the stock gate. A stock gate is a cattle grid to prevent livestock from wandering onto the road and getting lost or going into dangerous areas. I unlocked the heavy metal gate and then jumped back into the car. We came to a hill, so Dad slowed down because it was steep and had sharp curves. There were thick clouds of dust that day, making it almost impossible to see the yellow fields of hay. Dad said the driveway was almost two miles long, so it took us a long time to arrive. When we did, my sisters and brothers jumped out of the car. They'd had enough of sitting in a hot car with no air conditioning.

Aunt Nellie's house was tall, with three turrets and round church-shaped windows on each side. The attic had a diamond-shaped stained-glass window. She made a place for us to play in the attic. There was an old table with four chairs up there, so we played board games. We also played with the many stored toys. Even on cold winter days, the sunshine made glittering prisms on the attic walls. It was fun to watch patterns of colours dance around the room, sparking and twinkling off cobwebs and dusty corners. Every time we went up to the attic, Sandra and Earl asked,
"Why do the walls sparkle?"

"Because the sun makes prisms through the windows," I'd tell them.

There was a large white porch wrapping all around the front of Aunt Nellie's house, with green ivy crawling in and out of the white wooden lattice that Uncle Fred had so carefully put into place. He'd also attached a screen all around the porch to keep bugs out at night so they could sit on the porch to cool down on hot summer nights. There were several white lawn chairs on the porch as well. They had puffy red and white pillows on them, and at the end of the porch, there was a white wicker bench with a long pillow on it. Every time I sat on it, I wanted to fall asleep because it was so comfortable. Aunt Nellie did a lot of knitting and kept her wool and knitting needles in a large basket beside her rocking chair. She made us all snuggly sweaters for winter and special red and green ones for Christmas.

Every night, Uncle Fred and Aunt Nellie sat on their rocking chairs, chatting and watching the fireflies flickering in the cool summer air. There were so many different sounds of the night to listen to, including singing crickets, bullfrogs and owls. Uncle Fred liked to talk about the northern lights radiating vibrant shades of rose pinks and pale green colours flickering and flashing through the faraway northern skies. They were like ballet dancers moving in slow motion.

Aunt Nellie was standing on the front porch to greet us as soon as we arrived. She was tall, like my mom and placed her hands on her hips in a welcoming gesture. Her cheeks were pink from the cool breeze, and she wore a beaded beret on her silvery-grey wavy hair. She always wore a flowered dress and a fresh white apron with two large pockets in the front. She made her own aprons. She also wore brown leggings and brown oxford shoes with thick block heels. She smiled and welcomed us warmly with hugs as we all crowded around her. Aunt Nellie always made us feel welcome and I never saw her get mad, upset or angry.

As soon as we were inside the house, Mom handed Aunt Nellie the lemon cake with vanilla cream icing she'd baked in her best cake pan wrapped in a red-checkered cloth inside a wicker basket. It was the same basket we used for fried chicken when we went on our large family picnics. Aunt Nellie thanked her and placed the cake on top of the kitchen counter.

"It is so great to see you," said Nellie. "Let's relax on the front porch while supper is cooking. We're having roast chicken, mashed potatoes with gravy and fresh vegetables from the garden. I also made your dad's favourite apple pie with a cinnamon brown sugar crust. Uncle Fred made ice cream for the pie and churned butter for fresh buns."

"Aunt Nellie, I can't wait for dinner," I said.

She laughed, "You sound as if you never get fed at home."

"Where's Uncle Fred?" Mom asked.

"He's sleeping in his chair beside the fire. Last night was rough for him as he was coughing all night," replied Nellie.

I went into the living room and took my shoes off. The carpet was soft and warm under my feet. I asked my mom why Aunt Nellie's carpet felt so much thicker than ours.

"Because there aren't six kids with feet running back and forth on them all day," she stated.

Uncle Fred was sitting in his wooden rocking chair beside the fireplace snoring. I nudged his leg, and he opened his eyes looking startled.

"What do you want?" he said in a crabby voice.

"We came to visit you and Aunt Nellie," I replied.

"Okay," he muttered as the snoring began again. I touched his soft, pink hand resting on the arm of the chair.

"Uncle Fred, I'm going outside," I said, even though I knew he wouldn't hear me.

Dad once told me a story about Uncle Fred. He was in a war prison camp for three years. The prisoners weren't fed enough food every day and were sick all the time. Some of his teeth fell out, and some of the prisoners died from malnutrition and bad treatment. When Uncle Fred returned to Canada, he was skin and bones. His Mother and father died, and his wife died of pneumonia when he was at war.

Aunt Nellie lived on the farm at that time and told Fred to come home because there was lots of room in her big old house. She told my siblings that Uncle Fred enjoyed their visits.

"He's getting older and doesn't mean to be impatient she said, "He's just tired."

Uncle Fred built a wooden swing and painted it white to match the white porch and window frames on the house. The swing was under a huge tree with drooping green branches providing shade. Two people could easily sit on it. We all enjoyed sitting on it, sometimes arguing about who was going to go first.

I looked up at the huge windmill majestically towering above the house while a warm, gentle breeze slowly turned the worn-out brown blades with a rhythmic creaking sound.

"Why are there windmills?" I asked. Aunt Nellie rocked in the swing with my mom. She looked up thoughtfully.

"Windmills today have metal blades that harness the power of the wind," she said. "They have a number of blades that spin around when the wind blows on them and can be used to grind grain into flour, pump water or produce electricity. You're thirteen now and will understand more about windmills when you get older."

Sheryl, Kenneth, Sandra, Earl and I ran across the yard past the well directly to the barn door. There was an orange mother cat with her four kittens resting in the sunshine.

I looked at all the hay sticking out of the barn window above. Dad had tied a rope to the rafters in the hayloft so we could swing and jump into the haystack. It was an older barn painted red with white trim and carried a sweet aroma of straw and cows.

The chicken coop was painted yellow and reminded me of a cute little wooden house. I collected eggs every time I visited Aunt Nellie's. The nests lay across the back wall of the coop, and each hen had their own special nest. They were warm and rounded in the centre where the hens actually laid their eggs. I slowly reached into the nests, searching for warm eggs under the chickens. Some of the hens didn't mind, but some squawked loudly until I left their abode. Aunt Nellie gave Mom lots of eggs to take home for all the baking she did.

At that time, Nellie had four borders that lived downstairs. They ate a lot.

"They work hard all day in the coal mines. That's why their faces are covered with coal dust and their clothes are black," said Dad.

"Wash your hands," yelled Aunt Nellie as we stormed through the back door.

Mom, Dad, and Uncle Fred were already at the table. We sat down and bowed our heads. After Uncle Fred said grace, he raised his head and said, "Let's eat."

The supper was delicious. I loved the mashed potatoes with gravy, and if we ran out of potatoes, we put gravy on our bun. The turnips, peas and beans fresh from the garden were delicious, too. We laughed and chatted while we ate. Earl and Sandra were telling everybody about our antics in the hayloft. To end the feast, we had scrumptious apple pie with ice cream, which melted in my mouth.

When the meal was done I asked, "When the dishes are done, can we play in the barn some more?"

"Why don't you run off and play? Your mom and I will do the dishes," laughed Nellie.

We all noisily pushed our chairs back and headed for the barn. I could hear Dad and Uncle Fred mumble something as I shut the screen door.

We played for a while until Mom finally called out,
"Time to go; it's getting late, and you've got school tomorrow."

Aunt Nellie handed each of my brothers, sisters, and me a brown paper bag. I knew it contained her sugar cookies. We loved them because they were crisp white cookies with sugar sprinkled on top. We hugged Aunt Nellie and Uncle Fred, thanked them for the delicious supper and invited them to visit us.

"I need some baking supplies, so we'll see you next Friday," said Nellie.

We waved and headed up the hill with the dust blowing all around us. I'll always remember how Aunt Nellie looked every time she handed us the small brown paper bag at the end of our visits. She was so friendly.

A few days later, a letter arrived in the mail for each of us. Aunt Nellie had written her recipe for the sugar cookies on a white card and sent them to us. She wrote,
"This recipe is so you'll remember all the love we shared. Please pass it on to your own children over the years."

An important part of life is making memories as we go along and keeping them close to our hearts. I keep that recipe card tucked away safely between the pages of the cookbook Mom passed on to me. Every time I bake cookies with my children, I remember the wonderful days on the farm with Aunt Nellie and Uncle Fred.

**

Denise, Penny, Kevin, Joan, and Kenneth

Chapter 9
The Dance

On days with no storms...after the cartoons, I would run across the fields to play with my friend until supper time. On Saturday nights, we watched either *Sing Along With Mitch Miller* or *The Lawrence Welk Show*. This gave Dad an opportunity to show my sisters and I some basic dance steps. We'd stand on Dad's feet, slowly moving around the room, giggling to Welk's music. Dad was serious about dancing and keeping in time to the music. He was always patient with us, knowing he only had a small window of time before we got bored. There were times when I thought he'd forgotten I was on his feet as he whirled me around. He taught us all the popular dances—fox trots, butterflies, and waltzes.

Dad would give us a quick review of his favourite entertainers on the *Lawrence Welk Show*. Those included the Lennon Sisters, Bobby Burgess, and more great entertainers. Mom would invariably tell him, "Time to get dressed, or we'll be late for the dance."

Dad liked telling us stories about the family. Some of them revealed his compassionate side. One of my favourites was when Grandma and Grandpa were playing music at a barn dance. Dad's younger sister had polio, and he carried her and set her on top of the piano Grandma was playing. There was a banjo player, and Grandpa played the violin. Dad's sister sat on the piano with a big smile on her face, watching the people dance. Sometimes, my dad would pick her up and dance with her as she held on tightly. She was one of four sisters.

Most nights after supper, Dad would take his violin down from a hook on the wall. The one tune that gave me goosebumps was *A Turkey in the Straw*. It still rings in my ears and memories. Dad

would practice this tune repeatedly until he was satisfied. Eventually, my mom would say, "Leon, please put that violin away."

I was thankful to Mom because listening to Dad practicing night after night to find the perfect chord could be very boring. Other ways he entertained us included *(photo: Dad)* playing his juice harp, harmonica, and spoons or balancing a broom handle on his chin. That trick kept us giggling over the years. Over time, my siblings would take an interest in the guitar, harmonica, and organ, and there would be many jam sessions. Sometimes, we would get together with relatives, and eventually, music would be on the agenda before the night ended.

Once a month, Mom and Dad would go to a dance. Mom would then get busy removing bobby pins from her light brown hair and combing it into an attractive style using a rat-tail comb. She always wore a black skirt and a black Angora sweater. Then she would put on the white beaded necklace and earrings she kept in a musical jewelry box on the dresser. She would rub a dab of *White Shoulders* perfume behind her ears. Finally, she would put rouge on her cheeks, slip into her black high heels and check herself in the mirror. She would ask us to straighten the seam in the back of her nylons. Now she was ready for a night of dancing! I guessed she must have felt like a princess ready to escape the reality of being a mother and a homemaker for a few hours. My sister and I would lie on her bed, watching the elaborate process involved with her getting ready for an evening out. The whole time, we were dreaming of the day we'd be able to do the same thing.

My older sister Sheryl always made a big bowl of buttery popcorn and sprinkled it with excess amounts of salt. She would brew hot chocolate with marshmallows melting on top. Sometimes, if Mom had time, she would make divinity fudge to go along with the popcorn. Meanwhile, Dad would be getting dressed for the dance. He would wear his grey pinstriped suit with a crisp white shirt that he always wore to special events, or funerals. Mom helped him put his tie on while telling us,

"Watch me carefully so you'll be able to help your husbands with their ties someday."

Dad would put a dab of *Brylcream* in his hair to keep the shiny black waves in place while he whirled Mom around the dance floor. Then, he'd add a splash of *Old Spice* to his clean-shaven face. I would often gaze at him, thinking how handsome he looked, and wow—what a switch from wearing his grey coveralls. The only telltale signs that ever showed my dad was a hard worker were his hands. Oil and grease had stained the lines on his palms.

When my dad retired, he would help my mom wash the dishes, and those darkened lines eventually disappeared. When they both retired and moved into a seniors' residence, there would be many dances in the clubhouse. Dad always loved to dance and would spend the evening being a dance partner to all the widows, giving Mom a break.

Meanwhile, my sisters, brothers, and I would always prepare our nighttime activities. We would check to see what programs were on our black-and-white TV. Some of our favourites were *The Brady Bunch, Leave it to Beaver*, and *Gilligan's Island*. We knew we'd have to adjust the vertical and horizontal contrasts on the TV throughout the night, but we didn't care—it was better than playing *Monopoly, Snakes and Ladders*, or *Dominoes*. Eventually, we got 'rabbit ears' that sat on top of the TV, and when they were wrapped in tin foil, the reception became clearer. After that, we got a large antenna placed on the roof and it worked! That is unless it was your turn to go outside on a cold, dark, frosty Saskatchewan night in the dead of winter to adjust it. We would still have to manipulate the outside antenna until the reception became clearer. So, we devised a complicated relay system to solve that problem. The person standing in front of the TV would tell the person at the door, who would then relay the message to the person outside so they could turn the antenna with a pole that Dad had made.

We would usually spend the night eating popcorn and fudge, drinking hot chocolate and enjoying our favourite shows. Then I would head off to bed, sleepy and tired from the day's activities and snuggle under the quilts my grandma had made for us, wondering if they would ever wear out. Then, I'd close my eyes and begin planning new adventures for the next day.

***

Mom and Dad

Chapter 10
Heart and Sole

It was Saturday morning, and I rolled over in my bed. The sun was pouring into the bedroom I shared with my sisters Sheryl and Sandra. I could hear Dad clomping across the floor in his work boots; he was a mechanic, and garage odours always followed him home.

Dad always tended to his garden in the early morning. That day, I thought he had probably gone to the garden to get away from the chattering and disagreements of his five other children at the breakfast table. The garden was a peaceful place for him to gather his thoughts.

I got out of bed, trudged slowly into the kitchen and sat down at the table with my two brothers and three sisters. Mom put a bowl of hot porridge on the table for me. Judy, the youngest, was sitting in her highchair, entertaining us with her usual antics. I noticed that she was learning to use a spoon, dipping it into her porridge instead of putting it into her mouth. That is why it was going onto her face and into her hair. Mom scolded us for laughing, saying, "Judy will never learn if you continue to laugh at her silliness!"

My brother Kenneth pushed a bowl of brown sugar in front of me. I poured delicious cream from a white jug onto the porridge, then applied a large spoonful of sugar. It slowly disappeared over the hot oatmeal. We had porridge for breakfast, Mondays to Saturdays in those days. On Sundays, before church, Mom always cooked a special breakfast that included scrambled eggs, delicious sausages, brown crisp toast, and buttered pancakes covered in golden maple syrup. Mom made jam in the summer that was scrumptious with our hot buttered toast. I rushed through breakfast because there were still dishes to do before I left to meet my cousin Nancy. I ask permission to be excused from the table and was given permission to do so. My sister and I gathered up the dishes to be washed and wiped.

My brothers disappeared silently outside to play. I wondered why they never had to do the dishes. But then my sisters and I never helped a Dad in the garage when he was fixing my uncles' vehicles or shovelling snow in the winter. I guess we had it easy because we never had to get dirty. Mom was busy wrapping Dad's lunch in waxed paper. She'd made him two bologna sandwiches with mustard, wrapping them in wax paper and a slice of his favourite iced lemon loaf. I thought all of my mom's baking was delicious-- especially when it was covered with that soft, silky chocolate icing.

Dad came in the back door after his inspection of the garden. We never treaded that one place without his permission. The only time he would let us go there was to pick ladybugs off the potato leaves. Then, we would catch the ladybugs and put them into a jar to see how long they would live. I counted myself lucky that we did not have to pick any weeds as my friends did. Mom handed Dad his lunch bucket and a thermos filled with hot coffee at the back door. Dad then hollered, "Good-bye."

After we finished our kitchen chores, Mom came into the kitchen and took some coins out of her apron pockets. We each got a bi-monthly twenty-five cent allowance—exactly one quarter, or combinations of pennies, dimes and nickels. I liked the nickels and pennies because I could hear them jingle in my pocket when I skipped.

My cousin Nancy and I were going to the movies that day to see *The Lone Ranger.* This was, of course, with our parents' permission. I kept checking the clock to make sure I was not going to be late. I ran to my bedroom, picked out my blue jeans and red checkered shirt, grabbed my running shoes at the back door, and yelled, "Goodbye, Mom."

Mom replied, "Have fun and be home in time for supper. We will have your favourite, beef stew and dumplings.

Everything mom cooked was delicious. She baked scrumptious bread, sweet crusty desserts, and amazing fudges. She cooked tasty vegetables that came from our garden and tender meat from my uncle's butcher shop. The milk, cream, and eggs she used came from the neighbouring Bennett farm. In exchange, Dad gave old man Bennett vegetables.

Nancy was waiting for me at the planned meeting place. We started walking up the middle of the train tracks, giggling about stories of family or school, always looking back over our shoulders, listening for a train whistle. While we were jumping from one wooden tie to the next, I said, "I want to drop by and say hi to Dad before we go to the movies."

We arrived at his garage and looked around, but there was no sign of Dad. I could hear him calling my name, so we walked over to his automobile and saw him working in the pit under it.

"Hi, Dad," I said, "We just wanted to stop and say hi before we went to the movie."

He reached into his pocket and handed me a dime with that special smile of his. I was surprised and thanked him. The dime was probably for a soda. Nancy and I turned and ran out into the busy street and headed to the candy store. That store had been in the same place for as long as I could remember. At the entrance, right inside the door, there were little brown paper bags on the counter for customers to choose their candies. After we chose our sweets, we took the bag to the counter lady at the front of the store. She then decided to turn the bag upside down so she could carefully count the contents before putting them back into the bag. I'd bought a lot of candy and still had ten cents left. With that, I was going to buy a soda and a bag of popcorn to share with Nancy once we got to the theatre. We left the confectionary with our bags of mouthwatering treats, which included sugar-coated spearmint leaves, sugar strawberry candies, candy corn and red licorice. We called it penny candy because you could buy four candies for one cent. We crossed the street holding our paper bags tightly, walking towards the scent of popcorn, and entered the theatre, purchasing our tickets at the ticket booth. They then bought a large bag of popcorn dipping with hot butter and a soda from the concession, which I planned to share with Nancy.

We walked into the dark theatre and picked our usual seats in the front row as if they were reserved for us. As soon as the show started, we munched on our goodies and drank thirst-quenching bottles of grape soda. The whole theatre was silent as we watched the action of the Lone Ranger. Nancy and I enjoyed the movie, along with some noisy friends from school. After the show, we walked back down the tracks analyzing the performances, anxious to see the next one. I finally said, "Goodbye, Nancy," and hurried across the bridge that led to my home.

There were always several pairs of shoes stacked on the back porch. I took my shoes off and made sure not to trip. My foot caught on a shoe, and I stumbled but was able to catch my balance. I picked up Dad's worn-out boots, which smelled of oil and grease, held them for a few seconds, and then threw them back on the pile. I was shocked to see a hole in the bottom of his boots with a piece of cardboard stuck inside to cover the hole. It made me sad to see that he had to put cardboard in his shoe.

Quiet tears ran down my face when I thought of how he had given me his last dime that afternoon.

Mom called me, saying, "Hurry up before your supper gets cold."
I looked at my dad sitting at the end of the table. I had a very
special father and realized that he was happy as long as his
children had shoes with no holes. I was feeling very grateful at
that moment.

***

Mom and Dad

Chapter 11
School Days

"Hurry up, Kenneth, or we'll be late for school! " The bell was ringing as we ran to line up outside the school. The Principal, Mr. Harrison, was standing staunchly on the school steps, waiting for everyone to stop talking. Then he smiled and said,
"Good morning, everyone."

Grades four and five were in the same classroom, and our teacher was Miss Wilson. She was waiting for everyone to stop chatting so we could sing *God Save the Queen*. She was always my favourite teacher because she was pretty and never yelled at me or made me cry.

At the beginning of the year, she gave us our school supplies—one pencil, one eraser, and one scribbler. I asked her,
"When will we start to use a pen?"

"When you're in grade six," she replied while handing out textbooks with sheets of thick brown paper to make their covers. By the end of the year, my cover was plastered with pictures of hills, trees, doodles, and misspelt words.

The alphabet is printed in large letters at the top of the blackboard, and underneath the letters is a map covering the whole blackboard. The map pulled up and down when the teacher needed it. I would daydream about travelling to all the countries on the map.

When I was in Grade 12, I learnt how difficult it was to become a female teacher. Women made up the majority of elementary school teachers since 1880 but their initial acceptance into the profession came forty years earlier. In the 1840s, options for women who wanted to work outside the home were limited to subordinate roles such as domestic work or factory jobs. Women teachers of younger children were paid less than men and School Boards could save money by hiring young women for primary classes while offering higher salaries to men teaching the higher grades. When a man married, they received bonuses or promotions but when a woman married, they were fired and told to go home.

The suffrage movement helped open the doors for women to universities and the professions and resulted in women winning the right to vote in 1918. In those days, there was a belief that women couldn't contribute to political life. They were considered too weak, too easily led, too illogical and too emotional. They were also thought to lack the knowledge of how to vote wisely.

In 1888, eight women formed the Ladies Teachers' Association of Toronto, later called the Women Teachers' Association of Toronto. In 1919, they set $650 as the minimum annual salary and urged their colleagues not to undercut others by accepting lower pay. Women elementary school teachers found their working conditions better than those of many other women workers. More than fifty years of action by their federation had given them employment rights, such as the ability to get married and have children without losing their jobs.

In the 1970s, a new generation of women teachers found their progress impeded by ceilings on School Board budgets. Boards attempted to replace junior kindergarten teachers with early childhood education graduates. They increased primary class sizes and introduced teaching assistants to handle the extra workload. Special education programs were slashed, and libraries were closed. On many Boards, Library Technicians replaced teacher-librarians.

Throughout most of history, women have had fewer legal rights and career opportunities than men have. Wifehood and motherhood were regarded as women's most significant professions. In the 20th century however, women in most nations won the right to vote and increased their educational and job opportunities. Women's rights are the fundamental human rights that were enshrined by the United Nations for every human being on the planet seventy years ago.

Women's roles have changed in the last 100 years. Yet everywhere around the world, women and girls have been denied them, often simply because of their gender.

***

Earl and Sandra

Chapter 12
Top of the Morning

Sunday dinner at our place was always special because on that day, Grandpa always came. After supper, he would scuffle slowly to the solarium so he could watch the birds fluttering around the bird bath. He would tell me the same story every week about how our ancestors emigrated from Ireland. Grandpa told me he had a diary full of notes that had been given to him by his own grandfather. He also told us about the great Irish famine that drove thousands of sick and starving families to leave Ireland and migrate to Canada.

He told us that the year 1847—what the Irish called Black 47—was a horrific year for Irish people. Potatoes were the main diet for most poor Irish folks. Potatoes were being cultivated in acidic, boggy, and rocky soils. The crop was nutritious and, combined with cow's milk, provided a reasonably balanced diet.

But Grandpa told us that, in the 1840s, potatoes became vulnerable to a strange new disease. First, light green spots began to appear on the edges of potato leaves. These spots gradually grew larger and turned black. Soon, the plants rotted above the ground, leaving a terrible stench and turning to mush. Botanists thought the disease was some kind of root rot, because of the summer's unusually damp weather. They were wrong. The disease was a fungus whose spores could be blown across great distances and which returned year after year.

The pandemic that evolved killed many Irish immigrants and also took a toll on people we now call front-line workers. Though this occurred two centuries ago, the events of Black 47 have left an imprint on Ireland and Canada, linking both countries by strong bonds of genealogy and shared history.

In 1845, Irish potato crops rotted in the ground, and then they failed again the next year. Food prices rose. Wages fell. Tenant farmers could no longer pay their rents. Soup kitchens and workhouses proved insufficient to stop the growing crisis. Several contagious diseases, including typhus, erupted in Ireland. The county districts were in awful conditions, and whole families were dying at the same time due to starvation. Grandpa told us, "There were many other atrocities that are too horrible to talk about."

He read in his diary that between 1845 and 1852, approximately a million people boarded ships for England, Canada and Australia—to go anywhere that would take them away from their hunger. Approximately one hundred thousand sick Irish men, women, and children arrived in Canada during that period.

Grandpa would lower his voice to a whisper and tell us, "We had lots of relatives who died at that time because of the potato famine—either from the disease itself or from the terrible living conditions in Ireland in those days. It was so bad that many people died even before they reached Canada. The transportation that the Irish emigrants relied on was a system developed to export Canadian timber to the British Isles. Once the timber was unloaded in Britain, a temporary passenger deck was installed in the ship's hold to carry people on the return voyage to Canada.

With cost-cutting measures back, hauling people in this way could be almost as lucrative as hauling timber. In 1847, at the height of the Irish famine, more than 6,000 emigrants died on route to Canada. The ships that carried the Irish refugees were known as "coffin ships" because of filth, crowded conditions, poor food, rampant typhus, and high death tolls."

Grandpa would go on to explain how the emigrants lived on land and ships. Priests visiting one ship anchored off Quebec described how the Irish were up to their ankles in filth down in the ship's hold. The wretched emigrants crowded together like cattle and corpses remaining long unburied. By summertime, hospital beds were filled—often with two or three patients in a bed. Extra patients had to be moved to quarantine sheds. Through the summer and autumn of 1847, the tidal wave of emigrants and the typhus they carried followed the waterways into Canada. In Kingston, 14,000 emigrants died. Three thousand sick emigrants arrived one summer before the Rideau Canal was closed to prevent more from coming. Irish emigration to British North America peaked during the famine years and then dwindled over the remainder of the nineteenth century. In the 15 years following the end of the *Great Hunger*, another 114 Irish emigrants came to Canada, and in the 20 years after that, another 70,000 arrived. In total, from 1829 to 1914, 661 Irish men, women, and children entered Canada through the port of Quebec.

One time, Grandpa even pulled a piece of newsprint out of his shirt pocket to verify all his stories. We were shocked While we celebrate the Irish culture each St. Patrick's Day on March 17th, it's sometimes easy to forget the terrible price paid by Irish people during Black 47—not just the thousands who died or whose lives were shattered in Ireland, but also the hardships they suffered to get to Canada. Once here, they faced prejudice and ridicule and were labelled low, malodorous and unskilled.

***

Chapter 13
Fun at the Lake

Every summer, Mom and Dad used to rent a cabin at the lake for a week. We always looked forward to that week—but dreaded the four-hour drive it took to get there. To prepare for our holidays, Mom filled a wicker picnic basket and some cardboard boxes with food. She packed hot dogs and hamburgers along with lots of other traditional goodies. One year, she almost forgot to bring marshmallows but remembered at the last moment. That was lucky because there's no store at the lake.

"Let's stop for a picnic on the way," Mom said on the trip in the summer of 1965 when I was seventeen. She'd prepared a lunch for us to eat on the way, which consisted of bologna, peanut butter and jam sandwiches. Before we set off, she checked for food, clothing, air mattresses, beach towels and bathing caps. Most importantly, she put our sunhats on the front seat of the car to remind us to keep away from the direct rays of the sun.

That year, Dad and my brothers Kenneth and Earl jammed as much fishing gear as they could onto the car top carrier—snug beside all the suitcases up there.

I prepared myself for the long drive, picked up my colouring books and filled my pockets with worn-out crayons. I packed my jacks, some chalk for hopscotch, and marbles in a cloth bag that Mom had made for me. At the last moment, I grabbed my book, *The Bobbsey Twins*.

We had a bonfire the night before we left that year to say goodbye to our neighbours. Everybody brought food to the party. Mom made a scrumptious cake with my favourite caramel icing on it.

Dad, Kenneth, and I found some branches to sharpen so everyone could roast wieners on the bonfire.

Judy sat in the front seat between Mom and Dad with her arm resting on Mom's shoulder. Earl climbed up onto the back window ledge to get comfortable while Sheryl, Kenneth, Sandra and I sat very close in the back seat. Once we got driving, I got impatient and started to tease Kenneth. He told me to stop tickling his ear and pinching his knees.

"If you two don't quit, I'll stop the car, and you can get out and walk," grumbled my dad.

I was usually the instigator of any teasing that happened. Dad rarely raised his voice, so I didn't get too worried about his soft-spoken threats. I knew they'd never stop. I also noticed him turning his head toward Mom and grinning. It would take another two hours to get to the lake, and I would get very bored and hot. It was boiling in the car because we had no air conditioning. I couldn't wait to jump into the cool water.

"Can we stop so I can go to the bathroom?" I asked Dad.

His response was predictable. "Yes, of course, but can you wait for a little while?"

"Not for long," I responded.

"Let's stop and have some lunch," Mom said.

Dad pulled the car to the side of the road, and the back door flew open so we could make a quick exit. He then got the wicker basket out of the trunk. Mom took out a red and white checkered tablecloth and spread it on some grass beside the car. She handed each one of us a sandwich wrapped in wax paper. You'd think we hadn't eaten for days by the way we gobbled down the food. Mom made a large plastic container of lemonade and poured it into paper cups for us. Then, she gave each one of us a delicious peanut butter cookie.

"Let's pack up and get to the lake quickly now," stated Dad. "If we hurry, we can have a quick swim before it gets dark."

I smiled at Dad, remembering how he'd taught me to swim when I was five years old. After that, I loved to swim in rivers, lakes and ponds.

Finally, we arrived at the lake after a few more stops.
"It's getting dark," Dad said. "Let's get the car unpacked. Put everything on the front porch for now. Mom will put it where she wants it."

We all scattered, carrying anything we could lift. All I could think about was getting into the cool water after a long and uncomfortably hot drive. The cabin had a perfect location on the lake—right in front of the beach.

Mom smiled and said, "Everybody out of my way so I can get organized and then relax for a week."

I turned to Mom with my bathing suit in hand. "No problem, Mom." Then, we all grabbed our bathing suits for a short swim before supper.

"I'll meet you at the shore," said Dad.

I jumped in the water off the short wharf, which created a huge wave crashing into everyone close by. I giggled and swam toward Sandra who was having fun splashing Sheryl, Kenneth, Earl and Judy. They were wading slowly away from the shore, so they weren't impressed. We were laughing and splashing even before Dad joined us, sitting on the wharf.

We swam for another hour before Mom called us for a supper of fried chicken and potato salad filled with green onions. After the meal, we all sat on the porch in our pajamas, watching the sunset slipping down behind the tall green trees. *I can't wait for more swimming tomorrow,* I thought.

"I think everybody should go to bed now and rest for another big day tomorrow," said Mom.

Sandra and Earl were already asleep. We all shared a bedroom with bunk beds. Mom and Dad's bedroom was down the hall. Sometimes, Judy could hear an owl, which made her run into my parents' bedroom.

"Sweet dreams," Mom whispered to us from her bedroom.
I got up early the next morning. Mom and Dad were already in the water for a quick swim before breakfast.

Mom shouted, "Penny—I'll be up in a few minutes to make breakfast; please wake up your sisters and brothers."

"Let's take a walk after breakfast to find a good fishing spot," said Dad to all us kids.

"Great!" we all stated at once.

I turned toward Dad and asked, "Can we take a quick dip before we go?" By the time Sheryl, Kenneth and I got to the lake Dad was already lying on the wharf, enjoying the sunshine.

Kenneth was the first kid to get into the water. Sheryl and I followed. I was splashing and laughing at Kenneth because he looked like he was trying to get a breath. I could see Dad getting up while I swam over to him. He was flailing his arms and going up and down in the water. His face looked scared, and he was choking. I quickly swam over and held him under his arms, not knowing what to do next. Just then, Dad jumped off the wharf, grabbed Kenneth, and took him to the beach. Kenneth was still gasping. He laid him down on his side while Mom ran up to the scene with a blanket in her hands. Dad started to put his fingers in Kenneth's mouth to clear it while he rubbed his stomach. It seemed like forever before Kenneth opened his eyes and spat out more water. Dad kept rubbing his chest until Kenneth could speak again, and then Dad and Mom took a deep breath. Mom had tears in her eyes.

Sheryl and I stood there in horror, watching all the action, and turned to each other. I put my arm over her shoulder. Sandra and Judy were playing in the sand pit—unaware of all the emergencies that had just happened.

Kenneth sat up and looked at us. "What's going on?" he yelled. We all laughed, felt relieved, and gave Kenneth a big hug. He was only six years old.

Dad looked at me, "You're a hero today, Penny."

I'll never forget that particular trip and what could have happened.

We still go to the lake every summer.

***

Penny, a cousin and an uncle in the back. Mom in front.

On wharf: author's favourite photo of
Dad, Kenneth, Penny and Sheryl.

Chapter 14
Dreaming of a Red CCM

I was sitting in our sandbox keeping an eye on my baby sister Judy, as she kept stuffing sand into her mouth and then spitting it out.

I couldn't stop thinking about the red CCM bicycle I saw every day in the window of Franklin's Hardware on my way home from school. The large bright sign taped to it said, $20 and I knew I'd never own it.

At the supper table, I mentioned the bike to Mom and Dad.
"Our bicycle is old and rusty and has no fenders. The seat is hard and I'm always adjusting the chain when it falls off due to a missing link. Not only that but there are also spokes missing and a slow leak in the back tire."

Dad said, "If you save half of the cost of the bike, your mom and I will match you for the other half."

"How am I supposed to make money when I'm only twelve?" I replied angrily.

Dad spoke up, raising his voice. "That isn't the way to talk if you'd like to discuss how to earn money to buy the bicycle."

Mom commented, "I have some ideas. Maybe you could babysit, mow lawns, paint someone's fence, or walk a dog. As a matter of fact, Mrs. Smith is always complaining about walking her dog every day. She constantly whines to me about her arthritis and how painful it is for her to walk up and down her front steps. You could also look to see if any of our neighbours need help painting their fences.

I asked to be excused and left doubtful that I'd ever get that bike. I went out the back door letting the screen door shake with a bit of a slam.

Dad raised his voice, "Please don't slam that door, Penny!"

I walked down the steps, thinking about Mom's suggestions. On Saturday, I walked around the neighbourhood and knocked on Mrs. Smith's door. She opened it with a grouchy expression on her face.

"What do you want?"

I almost turned and walked away, but remembering how desperately I wanted that bike, I continued. "I'm looking for ways to save money to buy a new bicycle. I could walk your dog every day after school for 25 cents."

"Mmm," Mrs. Smith said with a smile. "That might be a good idea."

I was surprised; all of a sudden, she was so friendly. We talked for a while. "I'll walk Lassie every day right after school."

She then offered me a tall ice-cold glass of lemonade and a cookie with banana chocolate frosting. We sat on the front porch in silence. I looked around at all the plants she had placed in large brightly painted pots with little gnomes and dwarfs hiding behind them peeking their heads out. "You have a nice yard." I remarked.

Mrs. Smith smiled, "Thank you. I'll pay you 25 cents every day—as soon as you return from your walk with Lassie."

I ran down the steps making sure not to slam the white picket gate, waving to Mrs. Smith and calculating that if I walked Lassie for twenty days, I'd have five dollars. I was anxious to make money because Dad said he'd give me ten dollars.

When I got home, Mom said, "The Clarks across the street are looking for an occasional babysitter."

I looked at her and said, "How did they know I could babysit?"

She replied, "I was putting the garbage out yesterday, and Mrs. Clark approached me. I told her you were trying to find ways to make money to buy a bike. She will let you know tomorrow what days and times they'll need a babysitter. Mrs. Clark said they'd pay you 20 cents an hour and 35 cents after midnight."

I grinned at mom and said, "Thanks."
If I do all those jobs, I'll have four dollars, but I'll still have to make six more to match Dad's offer, I thought.

At supper, Dad said, "Maybe we could go down to the hardware on Saturday to talk to Mr. Franklin about purchasing that CCM bicycle in the window once you earn the ten dollars.

I was so excited! On Saturday, Dad and I walked down to the store, and before we even crossed the street, I looked in the window and saw that the bike was gone.

Dad looked down at me. "I guess we won't have to order another one if there are some in the storeroom."

We talked with Mr. Franklin, and he said, "There won't be a problem buying a bicycle, I've ordered more, and they will arrive next week."

On Monday, I left for school and met friends on the way. I told Frank and Ben that dad and I were saving to buy a CCM bike from the hardware. Dad and I discussed it at the supper table that night.

Dad said, "If you keep up with the jobs in three weeks you'll have enough to buy a bicycle."

I replied, "Yes" and smiled at Mom and Dad.

As soon as I made the ten dollars, dad and I walked to the hardware to purchase a bicycle. However, there was no bike in the window!

I told Mr. Franklin, "I have all the money to buy the red CCM bicycle. I can't wait to show my friends and go bike riding."

When Mr. Franklin walked back into his store, I told dad,
"My first ride will be racing along the trails under the deep green forest canopy with my friends close behind. Standing up on the pedals, I'll jump over huge roots from the ancient trees and race up the big hill only to ride back down over the deep ramps on it. Racing over the old wooden bridge we'll make the boards squeak because, trust me—we won't be riding slowly. "We will whiz through the deepest mud puddles we usually do.

Dad said, "One day that bridge will fall down because there are so many boards missing. It's at least a hundred years old, you know. Horses used to pull wagons over it to take supplies into town. Please be careful when crossing it."

Mr. Franklin came out of the storeroom and looked sadly at me. "Sorry Penny, it looks like all four bikes have sold—the one in the window and the three in the storage room."

I turned and looked up at dad and felt like crying.

Dad spoke up. "We'll get one when the next order comes in," he said.

"Thank you, Mr. Franklin," I said, even though I wanted to ask him, "Why did you tell us there'd be bikes in the storeroom and why did you sell them all when you knew I wanted one?"
Dad caught up to me walking home in silence and rested his hand on my shoulder.

I got up the next morning and trudged off to school, stopping at the end of the day to take Lassie on his walk. Then I went home, climbed upstairs to my bedroom, sat down at my desk and stared out the window. My English book lay open on the desk to an assignment that was due the next day.

Mom called out, "Penny supper's ready, please go and tell you father."

I moaned, "Okay."

Dad was usually in the garage fixing someone's car. I opened the door and saw him standing by our car. "Dad, supper's ready."

"Penny, can you bring me the orange screwdriver on my workbench? The car door is jammed," he said.

My eyes must have looked surprised with astonishment. Dad was standing beside the car holding a red and white CCM bicycle. It had chrome fenders, red and white streamers flowing out of the handlebars, a bell to warn people when I passed them and a chrome carrier behind the seat.

I stared up at dad, "How did you get that bike—Mr. Franklin said they were all sold?"

Dad nodded, "They were all sold out! I bought the one in the window. Mom and I wanted to reward you for working so hard to earn the money and for keeping your part of the bargain. You should be proud of yourself."

By this time, Mom was in the garage too so I went over and hugged them both repeatedly.

I looked up at them and said, "I'll run and get my money—this is the best surprise I've ever had!"

Dad spoke up, "Keep your money. You might need it for repairs."
I thanked Mom and Dad again, gently taking the bike from Dad's clutches.

When we were adults, my older sister told me it took Mom and Dad a year to pay for that bike.

***

Chapter 15
Special Times with Gramma

I could hear the squeak of her rocking chair as soon as the screen door slammed behind me. Gramma's chair rocked back and forth with the same consistent rhythm.

Sometimes, she fell asleep in the wooden rocking chair. Her head was leaning forward with her hands folded in her lap. For a minute, I was frightened it was something more than sleeping—then I heard her snoring. I walked into the dining room where she sat every day, watching the birds fluttering for fat, juicy earthworms or eating seeds out of the bird feeder. We watched the birds flutter in the birdbath, chirping loudly as they splashed each other. She often complained about the neighbour's cat chasing the birds.

"All the birds want is to eat seeds from the bird feeder," she yelled. I had never heard Gramma raise her voice before—but that day she did!

"One day, I'm going to tell Mr. Purcell to keep his cat out of my yard—or else!" Mr. Purcell lived next door. "How are you today?" She asked me.

"I'm fine, thank you, Gramma," I answered.

Gramma stood up slowly, bending over to move out of her chair. She grabbed her cane hanging on the arm of her chair. She was wearing a blue cotton housedress with flower designs and an apron with big pockets. My mom was always busy making special aprons for her. Gramma wore brown oxfords with square heels and thick woollen leggings. She had thick, beautiful hair with grey and silver streaks that shimmered in the sunshine. She pulled her hair back and pinned it in place with pretty barrettes. Sometimes,

I would brush it for her, and it felt like silk. She had soft pink skin and many wrinkles on her face—but she was very beautiful. Her name was Florence, but everyone called her Flo except her grandchildren.

When my other grandmother visited, I always ran into the garden and hid behind the tall pea patch, which hurt her feelings. Mom would always tell me, "Try to be nice to her —she means well." I would reply, "But she never has anything nice to say about anyone—even you, Mom! If she means well, she should talk nicely like Gramma Florence. Every time she visits, she tells me my bangs are too long and asks me why I don't wear skirts. I can't climb fences in skirts!"

Gramma looked at me and said, "Would you like to go into the garden today and help with the weeding?"

"Yes, I would. I'd like to check on the cantaloupes. They're growing so slowly," I replied.

Gramma picked two straw hats off the hall hooks and handed one to me.

"It's important to keep direct sunlight off our skin, Penny. I know you don't want any more freckles from the hot southern sun on your face." They will slowly fade away if you rub lemons on them.

I laughed with excitement. "Gramma, remember when I won first prize in a freckle contest?" She turned around to look at me and we both giggled.

"What did you spend your dollar prize on?"

I replied, "Candy, of course."

Gramma said. "Let's go into the garden now."

She always brought her wicker basket to gather fruits and vegetables. She took such good care of her garden. Once I asked her, "Why don't you enter your vegetables and fruits in the fall fair?"

Gramma replied, "I'm not growing my garden for a contest. It is for me and my family and celebrates the special times we spend together—as long as you don't chatter too much."

I smiled at her, "I really like being in the garden with you."

The garden was located on a slope behind the house. There were fences all around it to keep the deer out. When all the plants and trees were blooming, it was incredibly beautiful. Gramma planted flowers between the rows of vegetables and sometimes even right beside a plant. There were also apple, peach and pear trees, as well as huge blueberry bushes. Gramma used those berries to make delicious pies. She preserved all the fruits in jars every fall and kept them in a room in the cellar that was dry and cool. She also had a place to put her jams. The root vegetables are buried in sand and wrapped in newspaper that kept them fresh.

During the growing season, there were rows upon rows of tomatoes, beans, peas, carrots and pumpkins covering over two acres of land.

"Everything will be ready to pick in a couple of weeks." She'd say every September.

"Why do you plant so many fruits and vegetables Gramma?" I'd ask her.
"Well, when I was a little girl, we didn't have any groceries stores. So, we grew lots of produce to survive the winters and to give to

our friends and neighbors. In return, they gave us fish, rabbits, and loaves of bread. So, I guess it just became a habit that I don't want to break."

"How did you keep all the meat so you could eat all winter?"

"We cured the meat by drying, canning, salting and smoking it. Sometimes, during very cold winters, we'd wrap it all up in layers of canvas and dig it into the ice."

"What if bugs got in?" I asked her.

"Bugs couldn't get into the ice—they'd freeze and die very quickly if they tried. But did you know the cucumber vines will choke out the other vegetables if we don't stop them," she said.

"No, I didn't know that," I replied.

Gramma then walked over to check the crawling cucumber plants that were trying to invade the tomatoes. As she did so, I noticed there were rows of juicy red strawberries ready to be picked. I helped Gramma pick the ripe berries and place them into a basket. Sometimes, when Gramma wasn't looking, I'd gobble down a few lush ones—but by the end of the day, I'd feel guilty and confess.

"Would you pick a couple of cucumbers for me?" Gramma asked. "Then we'll put them in a small bowl, add a little peppered vinegar and leave them on the table to snack on."

I gently lifted the soft, prickly cucumber vines and placed two fat cucumbers into the basket.

"Now, let's pull some weeds," she said. "If you see ladybugs on the potato plants, you can remove them."

"Can I take some ladybugs home in a jar? I asked her. "Sandra and Judy like to play with them?"

"Sure," Gramma said. "Just make sure they don't eat them!

I stepped over the tall daisies between the rows and noticed that there were many pink poppies scattered all over the garden— some with petals shaped like daisies and some like roses. Weeding was fun, as I stared at all the gorgeous fruits and vegetables. There were hollyhocks growing up the walls of the house, all different colours.

One year, we gave Gramma a thick gardening encyclopedia for her birthday. She always kept it on the table beside her rocking chair. She loved to thumb through it, researching how all her garden plants could be planted in different places, shade or sun.

That day, in the heat of the summer, Gramma said, "It's getting hot, we're finished our gardening now. I'll water it tonight when it cools off. Watering in the hot sun only evaporates the water. We've got one more fruit to inspect."

Then she'd bent down, plucked two large cantaloupes, and placed them into the basket. "Cantaloupes are slow-growing plants, plants and require a hot summer. We checked on the pumpkins and squashes intertwining around each other. It is a full-time job taking care of them. I'll check on the cabbages tomorrow because bugs like to invade their leaves and make permanent homes there."

Then, she'd picked a medium-sized cantaloupe. "This one will taste good with vanilla ice cream, don't you think, Penny?"

"Yes—you're right!" I'd said.

As we headed for the back door, Gramma called out, "The lemons and oranges will soon be ready to pick from the greenhouse. We'll check them in a few days."

There were huge purple lilac bushes in Gramma's front yard. Their exotic scents floated all the way back to the alley. She always kept a fresh bouquet of lilacs in a glass vase on the dining room table. Poppies are on the kitchen table and the daisies could be found in a pink vase on Gramma's bedroom dresser.

I got the ice cream out of the freezer while Gramma cut the cantaloupes in half and removed all the seeds. Then I put a scoop of the ice cream in the centre of each cantaloupe half. We sat, talked and ate that delicious ice cream. After we finished, Gramma said, "I'm going to have a nap now."

As usual, I followed her into her bedroom and helped remove her apron and put it on a chair covered with a flower pattern. Then she laid down, and I covered her with a thick wool blanket.

"Would you read me a bible passage?" she whispered.

"Yes, I will."

"That would be lovely," she answered.

After I did the reading, it was time to say goodbye. I bent over and kissed her on the cheek. She smelled like a lilac tree—a scent on her I would come to love.

"Goodbye, Gramma, see you soon."

"Thank you very much for all your help today, Penny," she uttered quietly.

As I left, it was clear her face was full of peace. *I'll come back on Sunday right after church*, I thought.

The next morning, I slept in and was too lazy to even get up. Then Mom came into my bedroom and announced, "Gramma died last night."

I rolled over in my bed and cried for a long time.

All the special times I had with Gramma remain loving memories for me.

***

Chapter 16
Family night at the Drive-in

Mom and Dad surprised me and my brothers and sisters at breakfast one Saturday. They told us they were going to take us to a drive-in movie theatre! Sheryl and I smiled at each other because we'd enjoyed the last time we went. The movie was going to be *Old Yeller*. It was supposed to be a great show, but with a sad ending. We spent all day Sunday talking about it.

Earl and Sandra were playing catch in the backyard. Judy was only three years old and was with Mom in the house. Dad was at work, as usual. Sheryl and I were busy taking the clothes off the line while Kenneth put the clothes in the basket and carried them into the house for Mom to iron. We were expected to finish this job before it rained.

It was warm—typical for this time of year in Saskatchewan. And it didn't get dark until late in the day. We finished supper and did the dishes just like we did every day. Mom popped a huge bowl of buttered, salty popcorn for the movie and put it into small bags— one for each of us. Dad was busy putting some blankets and pillows in the trunk.

Once we arrived at the Drive-in, Dad paid one dollar for our car, and we drove in. He always picked the same area to park his car— in the middle of the grounds about eight rows back. Then he reached out, grabbed the speaker, and hooked it onto his window. He told us one night, a person drove away and forgot to put the speaker back, so it stayed hooked to the window.

Sheryl, Kenneth, Sandra, and I got some blankets out of the trunk and spread them out on the gravel in front of the car. Mom gave us the popcorn she'd made. Earl crawled into the back seat, and

Judy sat on Mom's lap, unsuccessfully trying to fall asleep. Dad got a large bag of popcorn out of the trunk.

Lively music blared about the snack foods available at the concession stand—hot dogs with onions, mustard and ketchup for only fifty cents, hot, salty popcorn for fifty cents and a sparkling Coke for a quarter a bottle. Dad brought a bottle opener when we were ready to drink. Once the advertisements were over, the show began.

Old Yeller was a large yellow, brownish, long-haired dog.
 After the movie, we played for a while; there was an intermission, so we all got out and stretched. Some folks got out of their cars and headed for the concession. There were long line-ups that became short very quickly. People bought hot dogs wrapped in shiny paper, soft drinks, candy bars and hot chocolate. A big favourite was the small cardboard dish with hot, salty French fries.

There was a small place in front of the big movie screen with swings, teeter-totters, and a slide. Kids would play as long as they could until the movie started. Once the movie started again, everyone headed back to their cars. Dad brought us some surprise treats from home—chips in small paper. Some of us ate outside the car, and we munched on our popcorn, swatting away the never-ending swarms of mosquitoes. When the show ended, we gathered up all our blankets and pillows and jumped into the back seat.

On the way home, Earl slept in the back window, cuddling his truck and any other toy he was able to bring. Sheryl, Kenneth, Sandra and I leaned on each other in the back seat, sleeping all the way home. When we got there, Dad carried Earl and Judy into their beds while the rest of us talked about the movie. Later, I drifted off to sleep, dreaming about our next trip to the drive-in.

***

Chapter17
Birthday Wishes

"Mom—I'm going to turn fourteen soon—and I thought it would never happen," I said to my mom one day.

"Enjoy your days, Penny; they go very fast the older you get," she replied.

After my birthday, things began to change for the better. I could now walk home from the movies at night with my friends without either Mom or Dad meeting me after the show to walk me home. In addition, I could invite a friend over for supper. At my birthday dinner, I invited Connie over. She was my best friend.

"What kind of cake would you like?" Mom had asked me before the supper event.

"Red Velvet, please, with cream icing and vanilla ice cream; it's my favourite," I responded.

Mom always made our favourite cake on birthdays. My brothers Kenneth and Earl always asked for chocolate cake, Sandra liked Angel Food, and Sheryl wanted a white cake with lemon icing. Judy liked all the flavours, so she was easy to please. She was only three at the time and usually got cake and ice cream all over her face and highchair. She always entertained us with her cuteness, making messes for us to clean up. If we found a coin wrapped in wax paper in our slice of cake, it meant good luck. If you found a button wrapped in wax paper, it meant you'd never get married.

"I don't ever want to become a spinster," I said.

"What's a spinster?" asked Kenneth.

"An unmarried woman," replied Mom. "An unmarried man is a bachelor."

Turning back to me, Mom asked, "What do you want for supper? You get to have anything you want on your birthday."

"I'd like macaroni and cheese with lots of ketchup," I told her.

Mom would use her good China, which was part of the dowry she had taken into her marriage. That's why she considered those dishes sacred. Beside each dish, she'd place a cupcake container filled with candy and insert it with an open miniature umbrella.

Mom made nametags with colourful paper and drew a picture of flowers, dogs and kittens—something she knew we liked. There were always some balloons tied to the birthday chair. She put straws in all the fancy glasses and made a sweet tangy punch that fizzed once ice cubes were put in. To make the juice, she squeezed oranges and lemons and added lots of sugar. Then she poured the punch into her favourite glass pitcher.

On Mom or Dad's birthdays, we made them breakfast in bed. One time, we picked a dandelion on Mom's birthday and put it in a saltshaker for a vase.

"How did you ever think of that idea?" she remarked.

"Sheryl and I thought of it," I said, smiling.

We put her breakfast on a cookie sheet and covered it with a tea towel. It was two hard-boiled eggs with daisies painted on them, toast, coffee and a sugar bowl with cream on the side. This made her very happy and didn't cost us very much.
"We can't afford the kind of parties I'd really like to give you," Mom would say.

I had friends in those days whose birthday parties were very expensive. My best friend Connie had her parties at a movie theatre, and all of us got candy, soda pop and popcorn. But she never got a cake, and that made her very sad because her friends always did.

My friend June had parties at her parents' summer cottage by the lake and we all got to sleep over in a tent. We'd roast hot dogs over a bonfire and eat potato chips and candy. All night long, I could hear frogs and crickets making loud noises.

Once, Dad told us some things about the traditional history of birthday cakes--
"The cake represents the joy and sweetness of life, and blowing out the candles is a way to make a wish for the upcoming year. The act of cutting and sharing the cake with loved ones symbolizes sharing our happiness and good fortune. In the fifteenth century, German bakeries began to market special one-layer cakes for birthdays and weddings. Almost every culture now celebrates birthdays with a cake to make the guest of honour feel special and their day memorable and fun."

One year, I invited my school friend Betsy to my party. She had two brothers and lived at the end of our street. The house had never been painted and was black, with boards holding tarpaper on the walls. Dad didn't like to hear the neighbour's gossip about how her unfinished house was such a sore spot in the neighbourhood. Betsy's house still wasn't finished when we graduated.

Dad told me, "Betsy's dad has been sick for a long time and not healthy enough to finish their home. He's unemployed, and his medicine is very expensive."

I didn't care how the house looked; Betsy was a good friend. We'd climb all over the brand-new combines in the lot beside their house. I was always surprised we didn't get hurt sliding down the shafts with rotary blades.

Mom made hot dogs and buns along with macaroni and cheese for me. The cake looked beautiful with fourteen candles. Everybody sang Happy Birthday loud and clear. After supper, my sisters and brothers chased me to give me the bumps. That involved being taken by the arms and legs and bumped into the air, then down onto the floor. They gave me one bump for each of my fourteen years, then one for good luck.

It seemed like there was always a birthday celebration happening in my family because I had so many siblings, cousins, uncles, aunts and grandparents. After my fourteenth party, I was impatient for a whole year for another birthday.

Dad taught us not to hurry the days along but to enjoy each family party and every day of our lives.

"Treasure every moment of your life," he'd say. Our paternal grandfather said the same thing, and he was 87 years old at the time. Over the years, I have come to realize the wisdom of this idea.

***

Sheryl (holding cake) and Penny

Chapter 18
Skating and Dancing in the Winter

It was always great having two weeks of holidays at Christmas. In southern Saskatchewan, where summers were blistering hot, and winters were frigid.

My sisters and brothers loved skating, so Dad always made a rink in our backyard for our entertainment once the weather got cold. We'd spend a lot of time on that rink over the long winter months—especially when our brothers and their friends played hockey on it. I always reminded my dad how much we appreciated that rink. I had so many memorable times there with my siblings. Sometimes, Dad would skate with us or grab a hockey stick and join a hockey game with my brothers and their friends. Sandra is still a good skater!

Sheryl and I would sometimes take a break from the backyard rink to go to the community skating rink. It was great there, too. The ice was always smooth, and we never had to worry about catching the toe of our skates on a rut.

Mom and Dad exposed us to many other inspiring activities. They taught us how to swim in the Souris River. I loved swimming and did it every time we went on a picnic. Dad taught me how to dance. I especially liked the fox trot and the butterfly. And learning the two-step and box-step would be dance steps I have used for a lifetime.

By the time I was old enough to go on a date with a boy and dance, the twist, jive, surf, and a few others were the rage. The bunny hop worked for anyone who couldn't keep to a set of basic steps. We just hop around the room in a chain of people holding the waist of the person in front of us. Sometimes, I couldn't wait for the dance to stop just to turn around and glare at the person behind me. But sometimes, you might not mind who was behind you even if they were holding on too tight.

My grandmother taught me how to knit mittens and hats. Then we'd wear them to keep warm and look fashionable. When we went to the community skating rink, we'd wear slacks and warm homemade sweaters.

The rink had a special hut for skaters to put their skates on and leave their boots in a safe place. There were benches all around that hut—but no windows. There was a coal stove in the middle of it so we could keep our toes and fingers warm when we took breaks from skating. The rink was encircled by a fence of whiteboards with one gate on each side. There was no adult supervision, and any disagreements or issues that broke out between skaters were settled within the peer group.

A small concession booth beside the skating hut sold hot chocolate and sweets that people had donated. You could buy them cheap, and the money would go toward rink maintenance.
I loved the music we skated to. It blared out all our favourite dance tunes as I glided around the rink with my friends. We'd take each other's hands, make a human chain and do the whip. It could be very dangerous for the person at the end of the line because the longer the chain the faster they whirled around. And there were always couples skating hand in hand in time to the music as if they were professional performers. That always gave the gossipers something to gab about. We'd skate until they turned the music stopped for the night. Then, the caretaker would clean the ice. Sheryl and I walked home, talking about all the fun we had and how anxious we were to get home to our warm house.

***

Chapter 19
Sunday Best

When I was a young girl, I thought I was lucky to attend two different churches. Mom belonged to the United Church, and Dad was a Baptist. The churches were across the street from each other on opposite corners of Maple Street. They both had tall, pointed steeples painted white. Their bells rang every day. Dad said you could hear them for miles. I loved the sound of those bells.

Mom would give me ten cents for the offering plate every

Sunday. I'd keep five pennies and put five into the plate. I was sure my pennies wouldn't be missed. My aunt and grandmother put sealed envelopes into the offering plate. I was sure they gave generously.

(photo: Sheyl and Penny)

I would sit in the front row of the United Church Service every Sunday morning. I liked listening to Reverend Steed's sermons because he spoke in a gentle tone while he told the children in the front pews a bible story. When I was tired of listening to him and felt like I was going to fall asleep, I'd run across the street and enter the Baptist church.

The minister at that church spoke loudly and raised his arms in the air, waving them around wildly. I liked listening to the choir there.

They always wore burgundy-coloured frocks and sang beautiful songs. People would clap their hands and tap their feet when they sang. As I entered the church, I could hear my dad's lilting voice singing songs like *The Old Rugged Cross,* which was my grandmother's favourite. It became mine, too, over time.

Mom wore her blue hat with a tiny brooch pinned to it to for church. She always looked so pretty when she put on her dresses. All through the week, she wore an apron as she did her housework and took care of the family. But on Sundays, she dressed up, and it was a treat to see. She was beautiful.

I'd squeeze myself into the Baptist pew beside my aunt and grandmother and stare at the tall, stained-glass windows. Aunt Betty told me they were called Cathedral Windows. They told the story of the main events in the life of Jesus.

Dad would look across at me and smile, open his hymn book and get ready to sing another hymn from the thick, burgundy songbook. My five siblings would be sitting quietly beside us, trying not to fidget or turn around to investigate the sounds that strange people made as they entered the church.

The offering silver plate would be passed along each row as the parishioners made their contributions. When it was my turn to put money in, everybody would look to see how much I was offering. Mom told me to ignore them because it didn't matter how much money anyone gave. She said it was the act of giving that was important.

Sometimes, the babies of congregants were dressed in beautiful little sweaters, booties, and hats. The minister would hold them up in front of everyone in the church as the mother and father proudly stood beside their children. Then, the minister would say a prayer and gently pour holy water over the baby's head. Mom told me the babies were being Christened. I never really knew what it meant at the time, and I didn't ask. She said all of her children had been Christened, including me. When the sermon was almost over, all the children were sent downstairs to Sunday school.

I loved the Sunday school teacher, Mrs. Turner. She was a happy person and always smiled. All the children in her class were busy colouring while we listened to one of the stories she read to us. We sat at a wooden table and enjoyed small glasses of white milk. Then, we all shared a plate of delicious cookies.

Mrs. Turner would hand each of us a piece of paper with a bible story on it. We'd take turns reading, and when we finished, she'd ask us questions about the story. My favourite story was the one about Jesus feeding 5000 villagers with only five loaves of bread and two small fish. I asked my mom how this could possibly happen. She told me it was a miracle.

Eventually, Mrs. Turner moved on, and we got another Sunday school teacher. His name was Mr. Thomas. He was nice, but I always missed Mrs. Turner.

Every Sunday, I'd walk home from church and stop at McGregor's Candy Store. There was always music playing in that store and lots of friendly people hanging around. The older men would buy cigars and cigarettes and take them outside to smoke. They'd sit on a wooden bench and chat away—talking about all the adventures they'd had in life. It was fun listening to them. Some of them chewed tobacco, had long beards and wore baggy pants with suspenders. Invariably, they'd tip their hats at any women that walked by. Beside the bench, there was a small tin, and some of the men would spit their black tobacco into it. I thought that was pretty disgusting and so did Mom.

At the back of the store, there was a large red cooler with the words **Coke Cola** on it painted in white. There were many ice cubes at the bottom of that cooler with many different bottles of pop stacked on top of them. My favourite was *Welch's Grape*. When customers finished their pops, they put the empty bottles in a wooden box beside the cooler.

Inside the store, there were rows and rows of penny candies in little brown bags so we could carry our treats home. I took forever to decide what I'd spend my five pennies on. My favourite choice was always the same—one spearmint leaf jelly, three red licorice ropes, two candy corns and one black licorice baby. I could buy all that candy for only five cents, and they filled my brown bag to the top! But by the time I got home, the candy was gone!

In the summertime, I went to the Vacation Bible School with my friend. It was a weeklong adventure: playing outdoor games. camp and we slept in a cabin with six beds and a teenager to supervise. It was fun. At that camp, we learned how to fish and swim. We also took turns helping the cook in the kitchen and played baseball and volleyball every day. At nighttime, we'd tell Bible Stories and drink hot chocolate in the main cabin

Sometimes, we'd have a wiener roast and sing songs while we sat in a circle around a fire on the beach, listening to the crickets and bullfrogs. Some of us ran to catch fireflies and put them into glass jars. Then we'd jump into the cold lake laughing and splashing. You could often see shadows of wild nightlife and look at owls flying overhead when they got curious about all the splashing. That would make some of us scream. Before going to sleep, we'd all say our prayers together, kneeling beside our beds before we finally fell asleep.

When we finished summer Bible School, we received a certificate of completion. I still have them turning yellow in my scrapbooks. I really enjoyed Bible School. However, after I turned fourteen, I never went back. But I'll always remember attending those camps, making good friends and having lots of fun.

I always felt safe sitting beside my father, mother, grandmother, and aunt in church. It was a place where families thrived and got great religious training. Every night, Mom and Dad would remind me to say my prayers before going to sleep, and I always did.

***

Sandra (back) and Judy (front)

Moving Along Life's Path

Kenneth, Earl, and Judy

Chapter 14
For Your Autograph, Please

An autograph book is for collecting the autographs of others. Traditionally, they were exchanged among friends, relatives, colleagues, and classmates to be filled with poems, drawings, personal messages, small pieces of verse, and other mementos.

They were popular among university students from the 15th century until the mid-19th century. After a while, they were gradually replaced by yearbooks. When I was 14 had an autograph book with a red cover and the word *Autographs* embossed on the front cover. It was a small volume with colourful, pastel pages and measured four by six inches. Girls usually had Autograph books. We wrote in each other's book indicating the date and signature of the writer. Usually, we filled the pages of each other's book with short sentences, poems, drawings and personal messages.

When I left my parent's house, I took a box of diaries and the autograph book that I found while organizing the attic and sifting through paraphernalia and spider webs of years gone by. I quickly breezed through the many diaries locked with small gold-coloured keys and put them aside with the idea of writing the story of my daily life that would be for my eyes only.

Flipping through the pages of the various books, "He is so cute, I hope he notices me," never signing so one of my noisy sisters may accidentally read whom it came from.

I reread all the coloured pages that had begun to fade over the years, sitting in a box in the attic. There was a picture of the band *The Monkees and a clipping about Bobby Sherman's hit song Here Comes My Baby.*

I had carefully glued newspaper clippings of the death of President Kennedy with a message from Lyndon B. Johnson.
"He believed in the capacity of the young for excellence and the right of the old and poor to a life of dignity. Our public life is diminished by the loss".

I hadn't understood at the time, but knew the passing of this president was sad for a lot of people and important to remember.

Where did the last fifty years go by? I wondered.
Education, marriages, raising families, caring for parents.

In the autograph book, I read

Love many
Trust few
Always paddle your own canoe
                              -Helen-

A photo of James Dean pops out of the weathered pages his divine rebellious look, the sweetheart of the era, tight blue jeans, crew cut, and a seductive smile. He always had a cigarette in his mouth and a package rolled up in the short-sleeved white t-shirt. He wore a red leather bomber jacket and was as always pictured on a motorcycle.

Almost every girl had a crush on him in my senior years.
Some would draw pictures or doodle words of love on textbooks and sometimes washroom walls.

One page was psychedelic scribblings around the outside
Alana from an artistic friend ...You were always kind with people......

At the time, the autograph book was just a giggle:

Those hands that do a great deed
To those that are in a great need
                              -    Jeanine-

A rich man rides in a taxi
A poor man rides in a train
But Penny rides in a tin can and gets there all the same.
Good luck in the future
                              -Wayne-

Our actions, thoughts, and regrets identify our lives. Memories have a fundamental role in life, reflecting the past as the past and offering the possibility of reusing all past and present experiences, as well as helping to ensure continuity between what was and what was going to be. Diaries, Journals, photographs, and writing fond memories on napkins while you sip coffee in a cozy coffee shop will help dump the bad.

Memories ....Life
Every page is filled with words, poems rhymes, verses, pictures glued on pages that are fading away or slipping down the page.

the boy
that you noticed less.
                              -Bill-

Most of the poems from boys are ones you wouldn't advertise but as I looked back and reviewed my autograph book, those verses made me chuckle and remember.

If I was a ball of fluff. I would sit upon your dresser and be your powder puff.
                              -Love, your sister Sheryl-
  Love from your mother.....................
                              ***

Chapter 21
The Good Old Times

At seven o'clock on a Saturday morning in 1962, my husband, Dave's father, called him to get out of bed for his first day of work at his new job. Dave turned off the alarm clock beside his bed. Dave was nine and shared a bedroom with his brother Gord, who was thirteen years old.

Dave had been hired to work a four-hour shift at a grocery store which was located just two miles away from his own neighborhood in the busy metropolis of Toronto. He got up, grabbed his jeans off the floor, and pulled a clean shirt out of the closet. When he was at the job interview, the boss had told him what to wear for work. He then ran down the steps to the shared family bathroom, hoping one of his sisters wouldn't be putting make-up on. He splashed water on his face, brushed his teeth with Colgate powder, and combed his knotted, brown hair, which sometimes went many days unattended. Then he went into the small kitchen where his mother was preparing breakfast.

Large cans of peanut butter and jam sat on the table. The first time they were used, his dad would pry the lids open with a screwdriver. Dave's mom gave each of his siblings a large spoonful of porridge, a slice of toast, and a glass of milk while they all sat around complaining about having to do chores on the weekends. Dave grabbed a piece of buttered toast, slurped down a glass of fresh cold milk, and, as he ran out the door, called over his shoulder, "See you tonight, Mom."

On his way out, Dave heard the milkman delivering fresh dairy products as glass bottles rattled in metal baskets. The milkman always wore a clean white uniform with his name on it. Dave's mother would put the empty glass bottles out every Tuesday, and the milkman would take them back to the factory for sterilization and refilling. Dave's grandfather had been a milkman in earlier days. He used a horse to pull the milk cart and kept the liquids cold with a huge piece of ice.

On hot days, an iceman would deliver ice to all the homes to keep the iceboxes cold. Sometimes, he would chip slivers of ice from the bigger cubes and give them to the community children, who often ran giggling behind his cart. The ice would cool them off nicely on the hot, humid days of summer.

Dave picked up his bike from the backyard. It was an old one with a basket tied to the front handlebars. Its paint was peeling, and the chain was continually falling off. But he had to have a bike to keep his job at the store. He had been dreaming about how to save money to buy a brand-new bike, but his wages were only one dollar a day and it usually cost him 25 cents a week to buy candy or go to a movie. He also wanted to buy his mom a new apron because she wore the same one every day.

Dave passed the junk man picking up all kinds of rubble that people didn't want, broken appliances, boards of lumber, household chairs and scrap metal. Dave's dad had told him,

"Sometimes the junk man will make things out of junk to resell."

Dave moved along, peddling his bike faster and faster because he didn't want to be late for his first day on the job. His boss, Mr. Eddy, might get upset and say he couldn't hire him if he weren't on time for his first day. He got to the store five minutes early and was relieved. Mr. Eddy greeted him with a smile and said, "Good morning."

He worked hard keeping the groceries in order, sweeping the aisles, and taking out the garbage. Also making up ten-pound bags of potatoes and running them to a warehouse in the basket of his bike. But three months later, Dave's family moved to the suburbs, and he got a job at a pharmacy. That job involved taking stock in the back rooms, keeping the shelves full, making sure there was always pop in the cooler, delivering parcels on his bike, and taking morphine to old war veterans. His dad sometimes told him sad stories about the war and how soldiers used morphine to kill their pain. When he made his deliveries, Dave would often see girls peeking at him from around the corners of their homes.

Years later, he realized that many of those deliveries were packages that contained birth control for the girls he knew from school. It was great when he got any kind of a tip so he could put more money into his savings account at the bank. All he needed for a new bike was three dollars.

On his way home from work, Dave could hear the cutler ringing his bell to let people know he was there if they needed their knives or scissors sharpened with his portable grinder for five cents.

When he became an old man, Dave looked back on the days of his childhood as 'the good old times.'

***

Chapter 22
Wheels Up

The phone was ringing off the wall. I was trying to wipe the chocolate icing off Sandra's face while she threw her arms up in disagreement with me, which knocked the cloth out of my hand. I picked up the phone, but it slipped out of my chocolate-covered hands and almost dropped onto Sandra's head.

"Hello", said my husband. He was in the Canadian Military Air Force, and we were living on the Military Base outside of Edmonton, Alberta, then.

Speaking anxiously, he said, "There's a Hercules 287 aircraft flying to Victoria today. Would you and the girls like to visit your family for the weekend?"

"Yes, yes," I answered. Then I remembered my friend and I were going cross-country skiing on that Saturday. *I'll apologize and take a rain check*, I thought, *and I'm sure she'll understand.*

When's the plane leaving?" I asked.

"In an hour," he replied.

"Wow, not much time—but we'll be there."

My husband replied, "Good, I'll meet you and the girls in the hangar; just tell the guys up front what the plan is, and they'll page me if I'm not there yet."

"Sounds good, but I'll have to get organized before we leave," I said, hanging up and finishing wiping Sandra's face. Then I called Tammy in from the backyard.

"C'mon Tammy—we're going for an airplane ride to visit Grandma and Grandpa."

She clapped her hands and said, "Oh boy, I can't wait."

I packed a small suitcase for all of us. It was only a two-day trip so all I packed were the essentials: toothbrushes, hair curlers and clothes for two days.

In those days, Tammy was eight and Sandra five. They were great little travellers. Having a father in the military, we'd long since adjusted to moving around. But this wasn't the first time they'd ridden on a Hercules. It wasn't the most luxurious plane to travel on, but the price was right, and, as far as I was concerned, we'd definitely land safely.

My husband met us in the lobby, and walked us out to the loading ramp, guided us to our seats and gave us each a hug before disappearing down the exit ramp. One of the crewmembers handed us earplugs. The plane's side door closed, and the crew prepared for take-off. Huge crates with equipment and supplies were all tied down and crowded into the back of the aircraft. There was a huge motor and propeller suspended on a piece of metal.

I gave myself some self-talk as I do every time I fly—until we were off the ground. Take-off wasn't my favourite part of flying.
Sandra looked at me with wide-open eyes, not knowing what to expect. I took her hand and said, "Hold on tight, honey; it'll be fun flying to see Gramma and Grampa. We'll be there before you know it." She lifted her head and pulled my hand closer to her.

My husband always said there were more car accidents than airplane accidents, but that never helped my fear of heights.

"Wheels up," shouted one of the crew members. I thought it was some kind of good luck gesture. The rest of the crew got everything in order and turned to smile at us.

"Hey, we'll be there before you know it," I said to the kids.
Tammy understood me and smiled back. Sandra was restless but she did smile back at me while squirming as she tried to lose her seat belt. I could hear the noisy propellers winding up as we started to slowly move down the tarmac, ready for takeoff

We sat in the jump seats along the walls of the plane.
One of the crew members was reading my mind. He mentioned,
" We won't be flying as high as usual. This flight is a practice search and rescue mission."

I moved my hand in a thank-you gesture. His words didn't help my fear of heights, though. I looked toward some commotion happening halfway down the aisle and saw a crew member preparing to sit down in a chair that had a clear view of the ground. I asked one of the stewards what practice and search missions were.

"They can perform many different functions," he answered, "Much of the special equipment used is quite unique. They include utility helicopters, armoured vehicles and standardized pallets for transporting cargo and military personnel. The Hercules aircraft performs search and rescue sorties, scientific research support and firefighting efforts for the government. There are basic and specialized versions of the aircraft that perform a diverse number of roles, including airlift support, Antarctic ice resupply missions, medical rescues, weather reconnaissance journeys, aerial spray missions, fighting duties, and natural disaster relief runs. Actually, the Hercules has many emergency roles. We might be bringing supplies or equipment to soldiers on the ground who require emergency medical attention so they can be taken to the nearest hospital. By the way—would you like to have a look from this point of view?

"Yes," I said, forgetting all about my fear of heights. I looked at Tammy and Sandra. "I'll be right over there, pointing to a specific chair. I won't be long."

Sandra was already starting to fall asleep. The loud roar of the aircraft didn't seem to bother her. And Tammy nodded her head to confirm that she'd heard.

"Wow, look at the spectacular view, Tammy," I intoned. "The plane's flying so low I can imagine reaching out and touching the swaying, emerald-green treetops. I can even see a train down there with black smoke streaming out, resembling a black ribbon turning and twisting. It's spectacular; cars look like tiny black dots. Snow-capped steep mountains are towering majestically as they peek at the sky. The snow and ice look like they've been carefully placed in all the narrow, deep crevices and on the high peaks. It all makes me feel so peaceful."

"Yes, it's just amazing," answered Tammy.

One of the crew members then mentioned, "Sometimes we fly lower, depending on the mission."

"I can't believe it—they can fly even lower, Tammy!"

I couldn't even hear the noises of the aircraft flying over the blue ocean. So many different magnificent pristine places on earth were being taken for granted. I got help getting out of my seat so I could look down and get a better view.

I'm so fortunate to have this opportunity, I thought. The girls were eating sandwiches from a white box, appropriately named Box

Lunch. I opened mine to find a delicious meal of tuna sandwiches, sesame-seed crackers and a dill pickle.

When we landed in Victoria, Tammy, Sandra, and I thanked the crew. They all smiled, and the pilot said, "See you Sunday."

I couldn't wait for the ride home on that very airplane—the Hercules 287.

***

Earl, Kenneth, and Sandra with nieces and nephews

Chapter 23
Listen to the Music

I slowly walked up the steps of the military barracks to the third floor. It was another military base and another time to look for a volunteer opportunity. Our family was moving from one military base to another for the fifth time in twenty-five years of marriage. This meant leaving old friends behind only to make new ones and seek fresh adventures.

As I walked down the hall, glancing into a large room, I noticed several shelves full of records and soundtracks. There was also a table in the middle of the room and boxes of index cards sitting on it in organized piles. It looked like a library rather than a storage room for books and records. Soon, I found the manager's office. The name on the door was **Major Hunt, 1450 CHCL Radio**. The door was slightly open as if they were expecting me.

Whenever my husband was transferred to another place, I volunteered for interesting jobs. This time, my hope was to get hired as a DJ on the Cold Lake Base Radio Station. What I didn't know was that the station was completely operated by volunteers. In this case, the Major was the only military personnel involved.

I pushed the door open, saw a man in uniform sitting at a desk, and knew I was in the right place. He smiled, stood up to shake my hand, and invited me to take a seat. I told the Major I was there to apply for the position of volunteer Disc Jockey that was posted in the base newspaper.

"Why do you think you'll make a good DJ?" he asked.
"First of all, I love music and have lots of time. I'm very versatile and energetic and always enjoy learning so, for me, this would be a fantastic opportunity."

Roger, I and our family had returned to Canada from West Germany just long enough to buy a house in Edmonton, Alberta. Then we were sent to Cold Lake, Alberta. My husband had to choose either to be posted to Quebec or stay in Cold Lake. Our daughters were teenagers and had many friends and relatives in Western Canada. They wanted to stay in Alberta so that was a foregone conclusion.

The Major noted how enthusiastic I sounded.
"We're looking for someone to cover the *Nice and Easy* program from one to four pm daily. Does that sound like it would fit into your schedule?"

What schedule? I thought. *My daughters are independent, and I'd still be on the base if any concerns came up at their schools.*

"Yes, I think it would," I responded.

The Major then explained all the procedures with the DJs.
"You sound like you'd fit into a live radio environment. Another DJ, Ted, will mentor you on three of his shows. All you'll have to do is watch him and listen to what he says. When can you start?"

"As soon as you want me," I replied. "I'm excited about meeting all the people involved."

"Alright, we'll see you next Tuesday, Wednesday and Thursday from one to four pm. Ted will be expecting you."

I stood and looked into the studio window and listened to the on-air DJ. Outside the door, I stared at the red light in the hallway. The DJ was busy talking to his audience and putting a record on the turntable. He smiled and nodded. I smiled back. I walked away from the radio station feeling good about everything. I thought about what it was like moving every three to five years, adjusting to a new base and dealing with all the complications these moves created for my daughters.

When my husband came home, I started telling him about my episode at the radio station. He listened knowing he couldn't change anything even if he disagreed. I always reached out to the community when a transfer happened.

The DJ opportunity would be very different. Over the years, I had managed disabled teenagers, served at special events, and assisted officers with administrative work. At least I never sat home with cabin fever feeling depressed about the cold Canadian winters.

I arrived at the station an hour before my training session was set to begin. Ted met me in the coffee room.

"Welcome aboard, Penny. I think you're going to love the job and all the people around here."

I followed Ted into the studio where there was another DJ just ending her show. I was nervous, thinking I probably wouldn't be able to speak. Ted sat in the chair in front of the microphone surrounded by turntables, eight-tracks, a phone and various pieces of paper.

Ted opened his program by introducing me and telling his audience that I'd be taking over the *Nice and Easy Show*. I listened and watched him talk. His voice was smooth and soothing as he spoke over the radio waves. He told me there were five DJs at the station, most of them military personnel. He explained what I could expect and what music I should play. Then, all of a sudden, a telephone rang, and Ted picked it up.

"I'm really enjoying your show," said a fan.

"Wow," I said. "There's a lot of stuff to take care of when you're on the air."

"You can do this," muttered Ted. "Are you ready?"

"Yes, I think so," I said.

"Okay, come and take a seat right beside me."

I put the earphones on, and Ted said,
"When this record is finished pop an eight-track in. They're commercials and give you time to put on another LP."

He explained how the music and the commercials gave you the down time to keep everything in order and queue up for another record so you didn't have any dead air.

"You don't want dead air, Penny," he said quietly, "Otherwise you'll lose your audience. But I think you're ready to go solo now."

Her first day on air was a little slow. Ted reassured her, by saying, "The audience won't even notice unless it happens too many times. Remember, you're only a human being and we do make errors."

After a couple of weeks went by, I felt right at home.
One of the other DJs asked me if I'd like to pull records while he was doing his Friday night show, called, *Rock by Request.*

I enjoyed being on the air. Other DJs complemented me, which added to my confidence. After a few months on the radio, another DJ asked if I would like to help him DJ at a dance for all the teenagers on the base. I agreed but didn't tell my daughters I was going to do it.

The night of the dance arrived. All the equipment was set up and three DJs alternated being announcers. Finally, it was my turn. As the music was handed to me, I spoke into the microphone— introducing each song.

Then it happened. My daughter, Sandra, was dancing with a friend when she saw me. She stopped in her tracks and gave me a smile, not believing what she was seeing. Her mom was on stage playing rock and roll music at her dance!

When I got home that evening, she wasn't sure what to expect.

"Did you enjoy yourself tonight?" asked Sandra.

"Yes, and it was great to see you there with all your friends."

"You were terrific, Mom, and I hope you do that again."

Over the next five years at Cold Lake, My daughters and I made many wonderful friends and collected some amazing memories.

***

Chapter 24
Sherwood Forest

While sipping a hot cup of coffee, I looked over the schedule of events for a weekend in Tennessee.

"Maybe the Renaissance Fair would be a good place to visit," I said to my husband, Dave.

"Yeah, let's go—it might be interesting," he replied.

Everything had to be interesting for Dave before he would even consider going. I usually didn't waste a lot of time wondering about how interesting something might be. All I looked for was lots of fun. But Dave was an accountant and thinks in black and white. I worked with homeless people and had to be more creative.

Soon after, we arrived at a packed parking lot. At the entrance to the Fair, a rough wooden sign was dangling from a rope between two trees. On it were the words: **SHERWOOD FOREST.** We were in the right place! I picked up a program from a long table as we walked through the entrance. Before we decided to come to this fair, I did some research on Sherwood Forest in the days of Robin Hood. It was a very eventful time, and the program highlighted the essential dates and events.

Once we got inside, I felt enchanted as I saw a number of characters depicting the historical period. There were brightly coloured Nottingham tents with small flags attached to them waving in the wind. They each had dark green backgrounds with red-crossed designs emblazoned on them. In the middle of the flags were white shields with the silhouette of a green archer. A man was standing by the entrance, giving a brief history of the era from 1450 to 1650. Robin Hood's principal hideout was called Major Oak.

The museum's path was narrow and had various tall, green trees draping over a rough dirt path that had thick bushes alongside it. They were mysteriously hiding some of the tents leaving our imaginations guessing as to what we'd experience as we strolled along. We glanced at many different displays. Some contained characters dressed in the costumes of the day, and one showed Robin Hood and his merry men.

Robin Hood's adventures were actually legends from English folklore. They centred on a skilled archer and swordsman who wore a feathered cap and dressed in green. The theme of his life was robbing the rich and giving to the poor. Over a good number of years, he cared for and comforted the sick, blind and crippled in their secret forest hideaways.

Robin's merry men were dressed in torn breeches, small caps and shirts with balloon-shaped sleeves. Their hair was long, and they had scruffy beards. They carried swords in sheaths by their sides, leather canteens hanging from their belts and carved-out designs of animals and symbols on their clothes. They drank ale from large, dented mugs and, as we passed by them, held their mugs up, welcoming everybody.

Robin Hood was in the background philandering with the fair young maiden Lady Marian. Her costume was a long green velvet dress with white lace around the hem and an opening going up its centre. A bright burgundy cape draped over her shoulders, cascading to the ground, held together at the top by buttons. Those buttons were made of metal and were stitched onto the cape with thin pieces of leather. She had a thick leather belt, brown tights, a greyish-green cap and a green ribbon embroidered around the edge. and brown slippers. A green ribbon was braided into her shiny, long black hair.

Continuing along the path, we ran into my favourite character—Friar Tuck. He was leaning on a makeshift bar with his jovial laughter echoing through the forest as he gobbled down his ale, holding a large crusty loaf of bread. He was one of Robin's closest companions—a jovial monk expelled by his order because of a lack of respect for authority. His large girth and religious garb belied his fighting abilities as a priest and a warrior.

The costumes closely resembled the garb that was worn in those days. Poor people wore clothes made of rough, twilled fabrics called fustians. A peasant had a long shirt, loose breeches, and leggings bound crosswise with leather straps. Today, we call them jackets. Some of the people wore costumes made of linen, which was possibly the most common material used. Coloured clothes were rare among the working class because they were difficult to keep clean.

Will Scarlet was another companion of Robin Hood. He was a skilled swordsman and Robin's nephew. He was hot-headed but loved elegant clothes and was often seen wearing silk. He was the most skilled swordsman of them all while Robin was the best archer and Little John the strongest staff wielder.

Little John was another friend of Robin Hood who served as his chief lieutenant and second-in-command. His name is an ironic reference to his giant seven-foot frame. He was a master of the quarterstaff and, in folklore, he fought Robin on a tree bridge when they first met.

I looked at the program and noticed that lots of events were happening. One was a sword fight with Robin's gang against the Sheriff of Nottingham and his men. The Sheriff was an unjust tyrant who mistreated the local people by subjecting them to unaffordable taxes. In a forest patch Robin and his men were running away from the Sheriff. They were quick and nimble, either swinging from low-hanging branches, hiding behind trees or crouching in tall grass. We enjoyed watching the Sheriff get close to Robin. I could barely see Robin and his men disappearing into the thickets.

All the actors started to return to an area close to the path. They received hardy claps from everyone watching. It was so realistic that some of the crowd scowled at the Sheriff of Nottingham.

Aromas of food were drifting our way, so we turned and followed the smell. Around the corner, behind some tall bushes, were several huge brown shabby tents covered in designs representing the colourful flags of Nottinghamshire.

We sat down on stumps and worn wooden chairs around a wooden table which had boards missing. We chatted with some university students at our table who were studying history.

The menu had all the different foods that were eaten during that historical period. The main fare was huge chunks of orange cheese and large loaves of delicious bread. People were also holding roasted crispy turkey drumsticks that looked good. There were also fried pieces of beef and pork with thick crispy fat served on a metal plate with scrumptious buttered potatoes and carrots. Thick gravy was poured over all the food.

Soon a waitress came for our order. She had a long dress with a white ruffled blouse around her bodice which looked very uncomfortable. Her shoes reminded me of the slippers my mother wore to dances. All the servers had long black hair combed back with strong pieces of twine holding them in place. We enjoyed watching Robin's gang drinking ale and wine out of large silver mugs as they gobbled down their food.

I noticed a large brick oven baking perfectly shaped loaves of bread. The bread was pushed into it with long-handled paddles. There were large cast iron pots hanging over an open fire with steam rising from them. I peeked into a pot of thick soup. That display was an excellent portrayal of how people of the Middle Ages lived. We ate a delicious meal and finished with a larger than usual slice of apple pie, sprinkled with cinnamon and sugar.

Dave and I discussed how much time and effort had been put into this fair. "The fair administration did an excellent job planning and implementing the Robin Hood displays, Dave—wouldn't you say?"

"Yes, they most certainly did," he replied.

"What did you like specifically?" I asked him.

"I really enjoyed the costumes, the jewellery and all the tents."

Just then, we saw a sign that read—
JOUSTING PERFORMANCE @ 2PM
COME AND SUPPORT YOUR FAVOURITE KNIGHT

"Shall we go see it, Dave?"

"Yes, absolutely," he answered.

Suddenly, we heard a trumpet announcing that the next jousting game was beginning soon.

"We better hurry so we can see the show from the beginning," commented Dave.

Jousting is part of European medieval tournaments where knights showed off their skills by riding against one another holding long, wooden lances.

Two knights entered at each end of the field. They sat on black horses with braided manes, lances, and swords by their sides. The sword was a knight's most important weapon and the symbol of his knightly status. Before drawing his sword, the knight charged his opponent with his lance lowered. He could also use other weapons, such as short-handled axes or maces.

The knights slowly started to move forward towards the middle of the field. They wore metal helmets and partial suits of armour. Swords and lances were their weapons of choice. It looked so real that I had to shake my head to remind me it was all just a fake show. The most famous sword was Excalibur, said to have been cut from a stone by the Legendary Arthur Pentagon, who was the ruler of Britain at the time.

The horses started running faster and faster towards each other. Both the knights held their swords as if to strike down their opponent. Then they turned and started sword fighting while still on their horses. After a while they simply trotted off the field and everyone in the audience stood up and clapped, cheering for an excellent simulation of jousting.

In those days, jousting provided knights with a practical, hands-on preparation for real battles.

Just as everyone was getting up to leave the stands, a white horse came prancing onto the field. He held his magnificent head up high and showed off all the silver tassels that ran through his braided tail and mane. While the knight smiled up at the people in the stands, we just sat and waited.

Then he got off his horse and placed his helmet on the ground beside his stead. He turned and called out the name Sarah. I looked around and noticed a redheaded girl standing up. The knight then climbed off his horse and motioned for her to come down and join him. She smiled and looked surprised, but she walked slowly towards him. Soon she began to run with her arms out until he caught her, and they hugged. It was like a fairy tale. He kneeled, took a small burgundy box out of his pocket, then stood up. "Will you marry me?" He asked.

Everyone sat in silence, waiting, but eventually she jumped up and down, nodded her head, and said, "Yes."

The Knight kissed her and put her up on his horse. Then they rode away into the forest. Trumpets played loudly and the crowd again cheered and clapped enthusiastically.

Everybody believed that Sarah knew nothing about the marriage proposal because it wasn't planned for the joust. It was a surprise for everyone!

***

Chapter 25
The Fig Tree

I heard the gate squeak open and noticed it was my neighbour Annette. "Good morning," I called out. She didn't have the usual smile that always lit up her face. Annette and her husband Will have been our neighbours for twenty years. During that time, we have shared a friendly relationship while respecting each other's privacy.

"Come and have some tea with me," I said. "I was just pulling long, stubborn grass out of my flower beds, but I can always come back and continue doing that tomorrow. Grow all you want, quack grass—but stay away from my roses," I added, looking directly at the weeds.

"You have beautiful roses, Penny, and I especially like this one," she giggled while pointing to Joseph's Rose of Many Colors.

"It' surprises me every time it blooms," I replied. "There are always different colours appearing on that rose, including pink, orange, and peach, and there's a perfumed fragrance on every petal. It even blooms into the autumn in some climates. Anyway, do you have time to join me for some Earl Grey Breakfast tea?"

"I love experimenting with different types of tea," she said, leaning to sit down on a garden bench.

Hearing that, I brewed some tea and brought the pot and two cups out to the yard, along with some banana bread. We sat under the apple tree Dave had been coddling for years to produce fruit that tasted heavenly. He'd finally won the battle as red, rosy apples clung to the branches while we waited for the green ones to ripen. Nevertheless, he worried that some sneaky black bear might climb over the fence and escape with some of those sweet, luscious apples.

I saw that Annette wasn't smiling the way she usually does. Her smile was beautiful and always brightened up our visits. I poured tea into antique China cups that I saved for special occasions. "Is everything alright?" I asked, offering her a piece of the loaf.

"I haven't been feeling well lately," she replied slowly sipping her tea.

I didn't ask her why—thinking if she wanted me to know she'd mention something.

"I'm sorry to hear that. Please let us know if Dave or I can help you with anything." We then sat and chatted about the weather. "It's been a wonderful summer with endless daylight and lazy afternoons," I said and then continued, "I'm ready for autumn, which is my favourite season." After that, we continued to sit and enjoy each other's company. There were brief moments of silence.

"Thank you for the tea and delicious banana loaf, Penny. Can I have the recipe? She asked me.

"Sure," I nodded, "It's my mother's recipe."

That was the last time I ever saw Annette. Her husband Will knocked on my door three days later and said,
"Annette passed away last night. She was suffering from heart disease and had a stroke."

"We're so sorry for your loss," I moaned.

I saw Will that week in his yard trying to take care of all the plants and flowers.

"Annette always took care of the garden and kept it weed-free," he uttered with a grouchy tone in his voice. He told me he is feeling guilty for not caring for the beautiful yard. He pointed to something new in the garden: a beautiful array of plants and bushes with a stone wall surrounding them.

"This was always something she wanted to do in the yard," he whispered.

"What a thoughtful gesture," I replied.

Will walked over to the fig tree in the corner of his yard. "I think I'll cut it down," he finally said.

"Oh no—you can't," I countered, "Annette loved that tree and I remember her giving us fruit from it." We always talked about it in wonder of all the delicious figs it produced as we stood eating one.

"Alright," Will commented, "I'll leave it and see what happens next summer. If it doesn't produce anything, I'll get rid of it."
"Goodbye," I said. "If it's okay, I'll drop by in a few days to see if you need help with the weeding." Four days later, I wandered over to check to see if there was anything Will needed. I opened the gate and turned to close it, glancing toward the fig tree. Tears came to my eyes when I saw Will sitting in his chair under the tree.

***

Chapter 26
Memories

I entered my mother's nursing home on my weekly visit, smiling at her friends sitting in wheelchairs in the hallway. Mom was sitting by the window, frail as porcelain, watching the birds swooping rapidly to the ground, looking for bugs. The wind was blowing leaves around from the maple trees outside.

She turned, held her arms out and with a puzzling glance said, "Who are you?"

I smiled and wrapped my arms around her. She'd mistaken me for her sister. It was a painful reality for me that Mom couldn't recall my name or even a single memory about me. Time had robbed her of all her family memories. That was sad because she was so dynamic and taught us so much when we were growing up.

Family Picnic

She taught us how to respect others and ourselves. She taught us how to have faith and how to trust and accept all of our life experiences. She watched us learn and encouraged us to do our best in life. She told us, "Wherever you are, whatever you do, whatever life throws at you, I'll always love you." She gave us so much to be thankful for. She was full of kindness and love.

But now she can't remember the many times she forgave us when we failed life's challenges. Her memory was slipping day by day. The final days with my mother were filled with pain and sorrow.

One day, she rested her soft hands on mine and slowly closed her eyes for the last time.

***

Chapter 27
Marching On

Dave and I live in a waterfront condominium with a view of Mount Baker.

One winter morning, there was a knock on our front door. *Who can that be at 7:30 a.m.?* I thought. I opened the door and was surprised to see an elderly man standing there who lived down the hall.

He smiled, "I'm your neighbour, Ken Curry. My wife and I live in suite 609. We've never had the chance to actually talk to you because we only pass each other in the hall."

"Would you like to come in?" I asked.

"Not right now," he said. "I was just wondering if you could do my wife Norma and I a favour."

"What's the favour?" I asked.

"Could you come to our suite and help us with our uniforms? We're having problems with our tartan sash and kilts."

"I don't know if I can help you with that, but I'm willing to come over and have a look," I answered, "I just have to do a few chores and then I'll be there."

A short while later, I knocked on their door. Norma Curry opened it and said, "Good morning—please come in. I'm Norma and we're sorry to be bothering you."

I stepped into the foyer and said, "No bother."

The wall was covered with framed black and white pictures of Ken and Norma standing in front of an airplane in uniforms saluting. There were many photos of groups of soldiers.

"We were eighteen years old in this picture, waiting to be shipped overseas. Pointing to another picture with a group of men in uniforms, Norma told me, "These were friends we'll never see again."

"Thank you for offering to help us. Ken and I are in our nineties, and our fingers aren't as nimble as they used to be."

"We're going to a war veteran's ceremony in one hour and are struggling with our uniforms."

I followed Norma along the hallway. Ken was standing in the bedroom trying to put a tartan sash over his shoulder and pin a brooch to hold it in place. I fastened the brooch and helped Norma put her uniform on. Once they were happy with their outfits, they repeatedly thanked me. They were about to attend a ceremony honoring WWII veterans. They looked grand in their tartan sashes, pleated kilts, shiny oxford shoes, and military caps. I was glad I could help them.

A few days later Ken and Norma asked Dave and I over for tea. As time went by, we became friends with them and enjoyed listening to their many interesting military stories.

Ken had been in the infantry and Norma worked on Spitfire planes. They joined the army when they were very young and married two years later.

As we got to know them better, we learned about Ken's many war experiences. One of them was very disturbing.

"Can I tell you about the raid at Dieppe," he said one day.

"Yes, or course," I replied.

"When our boats landed and dropped ramps, we were exposed to a hail of bullets, shrapnel, and machine gun fire. We barely had time to set up our mortars because bullets were flying through the air from every direction," he continued. "I thought I was going to die because I could see many of my friends lying dead on the beach. Others were wounded, their arms waving, legs missing and faces burnt. I have no words to describe the pain and horror that was happening around me as I watched my comrades pray for a miracle. When I tried to return to my landing craft, I found it covered with the dead bodies of friends who were lying in pools of blood. They never even had a chance to leave the boat. I ran into the water, shed my uniform, and stayed close to the beach so the enemy wouldn't recognize me. Finally, the gunshots stopped, I fell asleep. When I woke up, I was looking at a German soldier holding a gun to my face. After that, I spent three years in a horrific prisoner of war camp. Conditions were intolerable. We experienced starvation, disease and the constant threat of sadistic guards. Luckily, my brother was in the same camp. When I found him, we held each other, cried, and felt grateful that we were at least together in this terrible situation. Rations were meagre. The men had to work, often at heavy labour. We were beaten and given very little food."

"Why did our mother ever tell us it was okay to go overseas?" he asked me after a pause.

It turned out that Ken was the last living veteran of the raid on Dieppe. Of the 582 members in his Unit, 197 were killed on the beach. All the others became prisoners of war. Only 211 ever returned to England and half of them had been injured.

Ken had joined the Royal Hamilton Light Infantry at the tender age of 15. He'd lied so he could fight. The minimum age was actually 16. All his buddies were heading overseas, and he wanted to join them. So, he did.

"After three years in that POW camp, we had to march for days to reach another camp," he said with a tear in his eye. "But Allied aircraft were flying above us so all the prisoners jumped into the bushes to hide. When it was all over, we stuck our heads up and saw that all the Germans were either dead or gone. We walked to a small town looking very tattered and thin. The mayor came out to meet us. Soon after we were fed, clothed, and slept for 24 hours."

I later found out through my research that the raid on Dieppe was a complete historical disaster. Over half the Allied forces were injured, killed, or captured. For the American forces, Dieppe marked the beginning of US involvement in European ground combat. At that point, their first painful losses were just getting started.

When he finished talking, Ken handed me a piece of parchment paper with a poem typed on it. I'll always treasure that piece of paper. It read--

In Flanders Fields
By John McCrae

In Flanders fields the poppies blow
Between the crosses, row on row,
That mark our place; and in the sky
The larks, still bravely singing, fly
Scarce heard amid the guns below.

We are the dead. Short days ago
We lived, felt dawn, saw sunset glow,
Loved, and were loved, and now we lie
In Flanders fields.

Take up our quarrel with the foe:
To you from failing hands we throw
The torch; be yours to hold it high.
If ye break faith with us who die
We shall not sleep, though poppies grow
In Flanders fields.

***

Fictions and Articles

Sooke Spit

Chapter 28
Penny's Points to Ponder

(Originally written for my 1980s column in the Canadian Forces Base Cold Lake, Alberta newspaper.)

Living in northern Alberta, most of us are not looking forward to the next months of seclusion with all that white stuff surrounding us. If you have got small ones, sometimes getting out is difficult or almost impossible when it snows. Here are some ideas that might help you pass the time a little faster during the long months ahead.

First, take advantage of the facilities offered on the base itself such as the swimming pool. Give them a call at 8194 and I'm sure they'll accommodate you whether it'll be for a family outing or just an adult swim. And think of all the pounds you'll shed because swimming is actually a very good exercise.

Connect—Moms and Tots is another retreat you can access. It's held Monday and Wednesday mornings at the Centennial Center from 9 to 11:30 am.

For those long, drawn-out Sundays why not enjoy a matinee at the base theatre? After all its family entertainment at a reasonable price.

Don't forget our library facilities where all types of reading materials are available.

Plan and start a winter project. Maybe try a craft you already know or one you've been putting off.
Or better yet, why not invite a friend over who's always wanted to learn how to crochet, knit or sew. Then you can spend the morning with a pot of coffee teaching her your talents.

How about answering those long overdue letters to your relatives and friends?

Or spend the afternoon preparing a meal that's different than your usual weekly dishes. Feed the children early then sit down to a candlelight dinner with your spouse. With just the two of you, who knows what the evening will bring. And don't forget to call in a babysitter at least once a week so you and your partner can have an evening out—alone.

If you can spare the extra cash, visit a beauty salon and have your hair restyled or treat yourself to a manicure. That'll do wonders for your morale.

Make some special plans for upcoming occasions such as birthdays and don't forget—Christmas will soon be upon us.
I'm sure we could add to this list, but most of all, don't procrastinate in those jobs you started a few weeks ago. Keep a positive attitude about yourself and the atmosphere around you will generally be cheerful.

Next week I'll have some diet tips for all your health-conscious readers and share a low-calorie recipe with you.

***

Chapter 29
The Tree House

Three months had passed since Simon, Sally, and Peter made plans to build a tree house. Now, it was finally completed!

The tree house was situated in an old, secluded oak tree in the forest. Their fathers had built the walls, floors, and a trap door. Simon's dad was a carpenter and had donated boards for the walls. Sally and Peter's dads had built many houses so were able to put the walls, roof, and trap door in place. Simon braided thick rope for a ladder to climb up the trap door. There were four round windows on each side of the tree house.

Simon's mom had sewn some curtains with little yellow and white squares on them. Sally commented, "They'll brighten the tree house up." Simon and Peter looked at each other and smirked.

When their dads had finished working on the tree house, Simon, Sally, and Peter helped them pick up their tools. It was then safe to climb up the rope ladder to the trap door. Simon's Dad reminded them, "Be careful when you climb up the ladder and hold the rope on its side."

The tree house was perfect. They thanked their fathers for all their help. Peter looked at the fathers and said, "We've got something to talk to you about. We've made a rule for the tree house—no one is allowed to enter it without our permission."
The fathers agreed to follow that rule unless an emergency occurred, and all the kids agreed.

The dads walked away giggling and reminiscing about the antics they had at fourteen. If they built a tree house back then, their parents would have never known.

Sally found a discarded bell lying by a school garbage can and kept it on her bedroom windowsill for a long time. They hid that bell behind the tree house in a small bush, would ring it to let each other know they were there, and needed the ladder to be lowered.

It was time to furnish the tree house. They found some old wooden apple boxes in a pile of rubble at the back of the grocery store. They used three of the boxes for chairs, one for a table and one for a treasure chest. They covered the chest with burlap, so it was out of sight and used it for special trinkets and treasures.
Sally always brought a flashlight with her when she went to the tree house at night because it was much safer than matches or candles.

There was one more important task left—to name the tree house. Some ideas were The Dragon's Den and The Secret Hideout but not all of them agreed on those.

"How about, The Secret Hide Away?" she asked and both Peter and Simon agreed. Simon volunteered to paint that name on a board and nail it to one of the outside walls.

It had been an exciting day, and they were getting hungry and tired. Saturday would be a good time to meet at the tree house to talk about more plans, bring a lunch, and stay all day.

When Saturday arrived, they were anxious to explore the area around the tree house. They climbed up the ladder, put their lunches on the table, and sat down on the apple boxes.
Sally and Peter brought some posters and taped them on the wall. The tree house looked great.

Three days later, some neighbors moved into the tree house without permission. Two big silky spider webs were dangling from a corner of the ceiling. Three spiders were waiting on it to grab some tasty bugs for supper. The sun was shining on them—reflecting a shadow of the webs on the wooden walls.

Simon, Peter, and Sally decided to go for a hike, and eat their lunches when they returned. They climbed down the ladder one by one; checking that the trap door was closed. When they reached the bottom, they jumped off and pulled the ladder back up under the trap door with another rope.

It was time for the hike, so they wandered down a path to the river that they had discovered earlier. It was dark. Some tall trees and huge moss-covered branches were hanging over the path, shifting gently back and forth in the breeze. There were twigs cracking in the distance and Sally moved closer to her brother Peter. All of a sudden, as an owl came swooping down close to their heads, they all jumped. Once the owl was gone, they looked at each other and laughed.

They reached the river and looked up and down the shore. That's when they noticed an old river boat that had paint peeling off and cracks in its windows. The boat was sitting on an angle in the water as if it were sinking. There were clothes blowing in the wind on a clothesline made of thin rope, tied from one side of the boat to the other. The name on the boat was *Catch Me If You Can*.

Sitting on a wicker chair beside the boat was an old bearded man who was fishing. He was dressed like a pirate with a red scarf wrapped around his head and worn-out sandals. His skin was golden brown and a long, gold necklace hung from his neck.
He turned and smiled at them and said, "How do you do?"

Peter, Sally, and Simon were leery of talking to strangers, but they slowly walked toward the man anyway. Curiosity got the better of them. His name was Fred, and they told him their names. They asked him if he lived on the boat and he said,

"Yes—it's my home. I fish, pick berries for my supper and grow vegetables in wooden boxes on the boat. If I need other supplies, I dock somewhere and get what I need from small towns along the way."

"Do you folks ever fish?" he asked.

"We did once with our father," Replied Peter and Sally.

"Have you ever fished Simon?" asked the old man.

"No," answered Simon.
"Well, would y'all like to learn how to fish? Because if you do, I can teach you," said Fred.

They all answered loudly at the same time. "Yes!"

They took turns using Fred's fishing rod. He showed them how to hold the rod and put worms on the hook. He told them,
"You need lots of patience to catch a fish. Sometimes it takes a long time but it's always rewarding when you finally do."

Fred explained how to reel in a fish when it struggled and told them, "If it tries to escape, hit it on the head with a club, and kill it before you take it off the hook." Sally didn't like hearing the killing part. He then showed them how to clean a fish at the edge of the river and throw all the guts back into the water. He put a fish in a black frying pan on a rock by the fire he'd already started. When it was cooked, they all tried some.

"That fish was delicious," said Peter and Simon.

"Did you like it, Sally?" asked Fred.

"It was okay," she said—not wanting to be rude and tell him the truth. She didn't like the taste of fish.

They sat and listened to Fred telling exciting tales of his travelling adventures. When it was starting to get dark, they said, "Goodbye Fred—we have to go now."

He replied, "Goodbye. Come back tomorrow if you want. I'll be here until at least noon."

On the way back they talked about how much they wanted to visit Fred and fish again.

They spent all weekend fishing with Fred. He taught them a lot about fishing and told them more stories about his adventures on the boat. He'd been a soldier in the war. "I hope you never have to go to war," he told them.

When it was time to go home, they told Fred they had to go to school so it'd be a week before they could see him again.

"It's important to go to school," he replied. "I went to school for a long time, and I became an airline pilot."

"Wow," they exclaimed.

They couldn't wait for Friday. On Saturday, they met at the tree house, played some board games, ate their lunch, and decided to run to the river to see Fred. When they got there, they were shocked. Fred and his boat were gone.

They were very disappointed at first but then noticed something lying on the shore where the boat had been. When they walked over to it they saw three fishing rods lying on the sand where Fred used to sit in his wicker chair. Above each rod their names were written in the sand and there was a note tied to one of them. It said,

"Two roads diverged in the yellow woods, and I took the one less travelled by…May you have many safe adventures in your lifetimes! Your friend, Fred."

They were sad they didn't have the chance to see Fred again and say goodbye, but they were very grateful about getting his note and for all the fishing rods.

They'd always remember the kind old Fred—a man who taught them how to fish, shared his exciting adventures and took them out on his boat—*Catch Me If You Can*.

***

Chapter 30
Save the Forests

The forests of our planet are beautiful and must be protected. When the sun peeks through the trees, it reflects brightly on the grassy grounds of the forest floors, exposing dormant herbs and wildflowers. Golden ashes, oaks and maples are anxious to show off their leafy foliage. Brown and gold autumn leaves rustle and carpet the forest grounds. Dense groves of pines with their slender needle-shaped leaves remain silent over all the seasons. They stand tall protecting their bounty of cones. Pine needle mulch is used as a growing-season soil to keep weeds down, retain ground moisture, and protect tender plants throughout the winter.

Acorns cling to oak trees with strength and endurance. An old rhyme suggests that if oak leaves fall before those on ash trees, we're in for light rain in the summer. However, if the pattern reverses, the summer will be very wet.

The fragrances of damp mosses refresh forest paths, welcoming spring with fleshy, rounded mushroom caps hiding in the shadows.

In preparation for winter, squirrels scurry to find scattered caches of acorns, assorted seeds and many types of nuts buried in nearby garden patches. With bulging cheeks, they scamper over tree branches, hanging on with their tails to deliver bounties of food to their newborn offspring. Big mammals that don't hibernate return to the forests. It's hard to imagine a forest without large deer and moose.

Some forest animals use trees and shrubs to shelter from the cold, harsh winters. Others help plants regenerate by eating them. They clear land for fast growth and help flowering plants pollinate and disperse seeds.

High-pitched chirping, tweeting, and whistling echo from the treetops as birds send signals when danger arises. There are thousands of birds throughout the world identified in many ways.

A bird's feathers play an important role in regulating their body temperatures and their ability to camouflage protects them from enemies. Some communicate non-verbally by beating the air with their wings.

Don't fight with crows. They can recognize human faces and are very intelligent.

Owls are beautiful, mysterious, intriguing, spooky and cute. Most of their 250 species are active at night. They can rotate their necks 135 degrees on each side of their bodies. They each have three eyelids—one for blinking, one for sleeping and one for cleaning. Some national parks offer evening owl walks.

Human over-consumption and expanding populations are the biggest causes of the destruction of our forests. The specific activities of mining, logging, oil drilling, agriculture, cattle ranching and war are very harmful to forests.

Trees are essential to life on Earth. We're destroying them so fast they'll be gone in a hundred years. That's why world governments must get involved in a crusade to save the beautiful forests of our planet.

***

Chapter 31
Hairstyles of the Sixties

Yesterday, while I was organizing my cluttered office, I picked up a yearbook that had fallen off the shelf. I turned the pages and recognized old friends and many changes to hairstyles over the years.

In 1960, with the formation of perhaps the most popular band in history, the Beatles were initially recognized for their Mop Tops. Over the years of Beatle Mania, their hairstyles changed and evolved.

Social movements were a large part of the sixties with the emergence of the Hippie Generation. Ponytails for men, shirts adorned with flowers for women, free love of all and the popularity of marijuana became the standard of the day for young people.

Twiggy burst onto the scene sporting a version of the pixie hairstyle with a sleek, smooth, boyish look. The Pixies eventually began opting for shorter, rebellious haircuts for the girls.

The Afro hairstyle became a symbol of African-American power, exemplified best by Jimmy Hendrix and James Brown. The afro was created by either natural-growing kinky hair or styles produced with chemical curling products. An afro comb was used to detangle hair that was tightly curled. It had separated teeth that were unbreakable but gentle on the hair. Afro combs are still used to this day by some black people.

The Flip became popular as the decade waned. It was produced by backcombing hair into a nest on top of the head with strands of straight hair resting on the shoulders. By sleeping with metal rollers in one's hair, a flip at the end of all that straight hair could be maintained.

Jackie Onassis became famous for her bouffant hairdo. The French word for swelling described a hairstyle that was teased, sprayed, and curled.

The Beehive came out when long hair was pulled to the top of the head in a cone shape and kept in place with considerable amounts of hair spray. The beehive was seen everywhere on celebrities, such as Aretha Franklin and in television shows like Star Trek.

Electric tongs and the new styling wand were used to create big curls with lots of lift. Some women still use foam rollers today because they're easier to wrap pieces of their hair. This was similar to women in earlier decades that used rags. Eventually perms came into style and with them women could avoid sleeping in rollers. People were using a chemical product "Toni" to perm their hair at home.

Hairsprays became popular in 1964 and were the highest-selling beauty product on the market. Men and women still use hairsprays today.

The first time I went to a salon was for my sister's graduation in 1967. My long hair was pulled to the top of my head and then shaped into separate curls called tossed curls. Bobbi pins held the wavy curls in place. It was a popular style for women with long hair, giving them a semi-formal look.

After sitting for two hours in an uncomfortable salon chair with strong-smelling products in the air, I went home and removed the tightly secured bobby pins from my hair, letting all the curls fall out,

Shampoos and conditioners were readily available at drug stores in those days. Today, companies sell hundreds of hair products, promising to turn women into beauty queens for a high price. Dippity Do was a sticky substance used to calm the curls and frizzy hair.

In the sixties, it wasn't strange to see women shopping for groceries with rollers in their hair.

Hairstyles will repeat themselves in a circular fashion as the years pass. Only their names will change.

Compared to today, hairdressers in the days of my youth charged very little money for their services. Those were the days, my friend.

***

Chapter 32
British Home Children

(This is a story about my husband's father, who was a British Home Child.)

The British Home Children were boys and girls from the United Kingdom who were relocated to British dominions and colonies in other parts of the world between 1869 and 1948.

During the movement of these children, over 100.000 British kids were sent to Canada from Great Britain. This child migration scheme was born during the Industrial Revolution and was motivated by social and economic forces. The orphaned and abandoned children were taken care of by many groups, including churches, unions, and charitable organizations. The boys and girls ranged in age from six months to eighteen years. Some of them were sent to Canada without their parent's consent.

For the most part, these children were not picked up from the streets but came from families who had fallen on hard times. Because there were no social safety nets to help them get through the difficult circumstances, those families had no other choice but to surrender their offspring to these organizations.

My husband Dave's father was sent to Canada in 1923 as a British Home Child, and he ended up working on a farm as an indentured labourer. Before he came to Canada in 1913, he lived in a Nursing Home. He went from that home to Fegan's Orphanage in London, where he received an education. He was then sent to a training school and taught how to farm in preparation for a placement in Canada.

Dave's father did remember that he had a sister. Paperwork had been incorrectly completed, indicating two birth dates for him. The children underwent medical inspections before leaving Britain and again before leaving the ship when they arrived in Canada. On the long voyage to Canada, they were kept in the steerage part of the ship.

Most of the British Home Children sent to Canada were hosted by farm families where they'd be put to work. The boys became farm labourers, and the girls did domestic work. When they arrived in Canada, the children were brought to receiving homes such as the Fegan Home in Toronto, Ontario. Their progress was monitored in the beginning, but as time went by, many of these children found themselves essentially abandoned. Siblings were often separated.

While some of the children were accepted into the families they worked for and were practically adopted, others suffered. They'd be reassigned to new families or moved from one farm to another. Some ran away or simply disappeared, and some died or succumbed to ill health due to neglect and abuse.

About 70 percent of these children settled in Ontario. Others were sent to Quebec, Manitoba, the Maritime Provinces or British Columbia. Between 1935 and 1948, the Fairbridge Society accepted over 300 children at its farm school on Vancouver Island. The children lived in cottage homes and were cared for rather than being placed in an orphanage. These young people were sent to Canada on the belief that they'd have a moral and healthy life. The organizations that sent them believed that rural Canadian families would welcome them as a source of farm labour and domestic help.

Many of the children were lonely and sad. Some were malnourished and others were emotionally starved and abused. They worked from sunrise until sunset. Some were as young as six years old. Many of those stories have been told and are heartbreaking to read.

Some experienced a better life in Canada than if they'd remained in the urban slums of Britain, trapped in poverty and held back by a rigid class system. However, when they became adults, these children hid the fact that they came from Great Britain. As soon as they left England, they were classed as vagrants or tramps.

As they grew up, some of them went on to own farms. Others became teachers, carpenters, doctors, nurses, merchants, secretaries, clergy, tradespeople, politicians and a wide variety of other occupations. Many enlisted with the Canadian and British armed forces during the Boer War and the two World Wars.

Dave's father paid for his indenture when he was 22 years old but he stayed on at the farm. Dave and his family are committed to extensive research of their father's origin, but records are very difficult to find. Events like World War II have destroyed valuable records. Today, over ten percent of all Canadians are believed to be descendants of British Home Children.

**

Chapter 33
Down and Out

George was homeless, and occasionally, after my early morning walks, I'd pop by Starbucks, pick up a hot coffee and stop to chat with him. Most mornings, he was slumped in a plastic lawn chair covered with a red tattered woollen blanket. The chair was close to a dumpster, sheltering it from brisk, bone-chilling winds. His blanket would usually fall to the ground when he saw me, and he'd lift his head, recognizing me with a welcoming nod. Grabbing the sides of his wheelchair, he'd struggled to pull himself along to where I was sitting. I could tell he didn't have much strength in his legs when he inevitably reached over to pick up the blanket without losing his balance.

"Here—you hold the coffee," I said while picking up the blanket and putting it on George's lap.

"Thank you," he muttered.

His hands were shaking, and I noticed that they were calloused with deep creases of dirt and grease. His face looked leathery under a grey scruffy beard and his eyebrows were long and bushy. His lengthy gray hair was also greasy, and his eyes were a haunting dark blue.

"Did you have a good sleep?" I asked him.

When the noise died down, he nodded. He'd slept beside a three-story shelter for the homeless.

"Why aren't you living in the apartments?" I asked.

"There's no space in there for me yet," he replied.

I glanced at the blanket on his lap and remembered all the extra blankets I'd thrown on the floor last night because it was too warm. This realization made me feel guilty.

So, I went into the trunk of my car and got out several articles I'd been saving for the Salvation Army. Then I handed George a coat, a pair of gloves, some torn blue jeans, a red tattered shirt, a blue flannel jacket, a crooked brown cap and some dirty running shoes.

He started putting the coat on, with a very appreciative look on his face.

"Here," I said, helping him get the coat on. I felt the dampness of the clothes he was already wearing.

"Thank you," he replied, shuffling through his new possessions. "I never remove my toque so I'll give this hat to someone who needs it."

"George, I'm a writer and I'd like to write a story about you. Would that be okay?"

"Why not!" he giggled under his breath, "I've got lots of time."

"Tell me about your childhood then."

"My father abused me and my mom. That's why she left him a lot—but she always came back. I hated my dad for what he did to us. I tried to get her to stay away so she wouldn't get beat up, but she wouldn't leave us permanently. She'd tell me that Dad didn't mean what he was doing and he was full of remorse. But the abuse continued, unabated."

"That's a very sad story, George. I'm sorry for you."

"It gets worse. My parents drowned in a tragic boat accident when I was fourteen."

"Oh no, that's terrible."

"Well, after that I went to live with an aunt and uncle who welcomed me with open arms. I got a job washing dishes after high school graduation. My uncle was a merchant fisherman, and he asked me if I'd like to become a fisherman like him someday."

"Sure," I said, "I'd love to work on a ship. After working in that restaurant for a year, I had saved some money. I told my uncle I wanted to do some travelling. He said I could work for him on his boat to save some more money so that's what I did."

"How did you like fishing?" I asked.

"There were many stormy days and nights on the ship where I got tossed up and down and side to side. However, they never frightened me. I loved the way gigantic waves splashed over the ship tossing it around the foaming sea."

"It sounds like you were a good fisherman."

"My uncle said I was born to do it because no matter how much the ship swayed, I never got seasick. But after a couple of years, I did decide to go travelling."

"Where did you go?"

"I went to South America with some friends and lived on a beach for two years. Then I went all the way to London, via Egypt. I made some money in England at a job laying the concrete foundation of a church. I usually travelled alone, but eventually met many people who became true friends. In some places I was tempted to stay a long time."

George started to talk slowly and look at me strangely, as if waiting for a reaction! I wanted to say, "Family strings had been tugging at me for a while. My uncle always welcomed me and invited me to stay as long as I wanted."

George preferred to wander on his own with no obligations to anything or anyone. He thanked the uncle who said he could stay for a while.

I asked, "How did your travels bring you to Sooke?"

"Over the time I travelled, my legs got worse, so I decided I better come back before I was too disabled. I've been homeless for twenty years, moving from place to place."

I knew that some of the generous people in our community were giving out food and spare change to the homeless, so I asked George, "Are you insulted when strangers give you money?"

"Not if they do it with a spirit of generosity with no self-pity in their giving," he answered, "The general population doesn't believe that the homeless people have any pride because we live on the streets."

George's father was a commander in the army, and they lived on military bases all over the world. Suddenly, he looked relaxed and started talking to me, making personal comments!

"When my knees get really painful, I wander around Sooke sharing my adventures with other homeless people. I go to the food bank every week and sometimes I like to give my extra food to others who need it more."

162

Every day he'd relax in his wheelchair in a different spot throughout town and then go back to his usual sleeping spot at night. George explained to me the four homeless peoples' rules for living.

- Don't move into someone else's space unless it's been empty for three days.
- Live by your own choices.
- Never manipulate another homeless person.
- Don't collect a lot of unnecessary junk—materialism isn't important.

Shelter and food were always on his mind when he woke up and before he fell asleep. All of a sudden, he was staring into space. It was time for me to leave. I asked him if I could come by another time to hear more of his stories.

"Yes, you can," he replied.

One morning, after one of my walks, I stopped to say hi to George at the homeless shelter, but I never saw George again.

Homeless Facts:
- There are 8,665 homeless people living in Greater Victoria.
- This includes 222 children under the age of 19.
- Research shows that 25% of homeless people are employed, at least part-time, while up to 60% shift in and out of full or part-time work.

***

Chapter 34
Risk of Game

"Why are you so late?" Tom asked Peter.

Peter answered, "I was helping my sister with her homework."

"Let's hurry before someone sees us," replied Tom.

They looked around to make sure no one was in the schoolyard and quickly ran up to the front door. Tom put his hand in the mail slot and reached the long bar inside that opened the door. They slowly moved inside the school making sure not to make any noise in case one of the teachers was still there. They paused, looking at each other. This was the third time they'd broken into the school.

"Let's go, Pete," motioned Tom as he turned to walk down the hall.

"Peter asked Tom, "Aren't you worried we'll get caught?"

Tom nodded and said, "Of course I am?"

They turned and started walking down the hall, passing the teacher's supply room. The first time they broke into the school, they'd ventured into that room with no intention of stealing anything. There were all kinds of coloured papers stacked neatly on the shelves. Glue, ink and rulers lay on the top shelves, probably so the younger kids couldn't reach them if they wandered into an open door. There were pencils, pens, and erasers in separate boxes on the shelves if students needed pens or pencils. Huge pieces of colourful construction paper stood in a slot on the wall, keeping them straight. Shelves of boxes full of textbooks were stacked, and large rolls of brown paper stood beside the books. On the first day of school, teachers gave out brown paper to cover the textbooks. Tom would draw pictures on the covered books' brown paper when he was in boring math and science classes.

Peter motioned to Tom and said, "Let's get going!" sounding stressed. They both ran and slid along a particularly well-polished section of the hallway.

It was Tom's idea to sneak into the school gym, so they went down that hall, stopping for a drink at the fountain as they walked past their homeroom.

Tom and Peter were both in Grade 5. The day before, they were given an essay assignment for the following Monday. The topic was—what do you want to be when you grow up? Peter knew right away. He wanted to become a professional basketball player.

"Why do we have homework when we're in school for five days?" asked Peter.

Tom replied," I want to be a pilot, flying fighter aircraft."

"I want to be a famous basketball player," answered Peter.

Tom continued, saying, "Of all the possible choices, I never thought you'd want to be a basketball player." Then they slid down the halls on shiny, slippery floors. Something they wouldn't dare to do on school days.

Peter quietly opened the gym door so they could slip in. Then he grabbed a basketball and started dribbling and throwing the ball into the net. They started playing a game as Peter ran toward the far basket.

"You're too short to score a basket," he said to Tom.

"Maybe," blurted out Tom breathlessly.

Peter sat down and asked Tom, "Do you like square dancing classes?"

Tom answered, "Only if Sally's my partner."

"Come on let's play for a little longer," Peter said, laughing at Tom's remark.

After playing for another half hour, Tom looked at his watch,

"We better get going because the janitor will be coming soon."

Peter nodded his head and picked up the ball, dribbling it over to a big box of balls.

Tom whispered, "Be quiet; I hear something; it sounds like a door opening."

Peter froze on the spot. Tom crept silently over to the window on the gym door. He then turned towards his friend and said, "It's Mr. Morley, the janitor. What are we going to do?"

Peter whispered back, "Don't panic." Then they crept under the stage on their hands and knees.

They sat there in the dark, afraid to breathe. They couldn't see Mr. Morley, but they knew he was nearby. It usually took him an hour to wash the gym floors.

Finally, the janitor left, turned the light off and commented to himself, "How many times do I have to remind those kids to turn the lights off after their basketball games?"

Once they were sure he was gone, the boys ran to the front doors and sat inside them for fifteen minutes before hitting the push bar and getting out quickly.

They ran across the soccer field until they got to the sidewalk.

"That was a close call," said Tom, "See you tomorrow."

"Maybe we should take a break for a while," Peter added.

"Yes, I agree with that," replied Tom.

They turned in opposite directions and headed home.

The next day at school, everything was normal. For a minute, they thought Mr. Morley might have noticed them. But soon it was Friday and Peter asked Tom,

"Do you want to go the gym tonight?"

"Yeah—let's meet at our usual place," he replied.

After supper, Peter hurried to school thinking Tom would be late. He was surprised to see him waiting for once! They were ready for another school break-in adventure even though they knew it was against the law. They decided that since they weren't going to steal anything it wouldn't be a big deal if they did get caught.

They hurried to the front door making sure no one was around. But as soon as they were standing in front of the school, they were stopped in astonishment because the door's mail slot had a board nailed over it!

At that point, they took off running towards their separate homes.

"Our school escapades are over for good," yelled Tom, over his shoulder, as he galloped along the sidewalk heading home.

***

Chapter 35
Buying a Home

Tom and Betty followed the agent into a house, smiling as they looked at the original hardwood floors and noticing the intricate glass doorknobs that dated back to the sixties. An arch-shaped brick fireplace with a unique mantle also impressed them. They'd been tirelessly searching for this character house! The living room was separated from the dining area with original French doors and the windows were authentic for their era.

"They've been well cared for, and they're not plastic," said the realtor.

I wish the salesman would go outside and let us inspect the place alone, Betty thought.

Their eyes opened wide with delight when they entered the kitchen. It was completely renovated in a modern style. It had a spacious look with an island and an extra sink—things that Betty had always wanted. It didn't take long for Tom and Betty to realize they'd finally found the house they really wanted. The bedroom walls were brightly papered and the bathtub had dragon's feet. The sun was shining through a magnificent stained-glass window onto a slate floor that had different flower patterns running over it. Tom could imagine relaxing in that tub after a hard day's work.

Before they could discuss a purchase, the agent took them to the attic by having them climb up a set of pull-down stairs.

"There are still a few things in here that belong to the previous owners," he said.

Tom couldn't see any water stains in the attic but there were a few cobwebs in the corners. Plastic covers protected some clothing on a rack and several boxes and bags still sat on the floor, covered in dust.

The double garage was also a bonus. It was somewhere they could keep their kayaks, bikes, golf clubs and other sporting gear. It backed onto a back alley so very few people would even know it existed.

In short order, the offer was made, and accepted Tom and Betty were the new owners and were then free from their high-pressure agent.

Two weeks later, they'd secured forty cardboard boxes and began the packing process. In three days, they'd finished bundling up everything and rented a moving truck from *U-Haul*. Soon after that, they finished moving and took some time to take a breather. Tom found some wine glasses and they relaxed on a couch in front of the fireplace, watching burning logs keep them snug in their new home. The next day they sorted through all the boxes and filled their cupboards and closets. A few leftover boxes were stored in the attic.

"I'll sort them out later," said Tom.

"That's fine, dear," replied Betty "And I want to put some winter coats up there too."

The following day, Betty pulled the attic ladder down and handed Tom the coats. He hung them inside plastic covers with the ones that had been left behind.

"This will protect your coats from mice and rats," he noted.

As he lingered in the upper space, sunlight streamed through a window keeping the floors warm. Spiders were busy weaving their webs and capturing bugs clinging to the webs for their dear lives.

Betty was curious to see what articles were in the former owner's bags on the floor. She carefully unzipped one of them and found a beautiful wedding dress. She removed it carefully from the bag as if she were carrying eggs. The dress had elegant patterns, intricate designs, a variety of delicate laces that intertwined around the waist and trailed down the back along with a delicate flowing veil. Betty wondered why anyone would leave such a dress behind.

"Maybe they just forgot it," commented Tom.

"I'm going to contact the agent and ask for the previous owner's phone number because I'm sure she forgot to take her dress," replied Betty.

Opening the second bag, Betty looked at a military uniform with stripes on the sleeves and shoulders, and four badges with brass buttons attached to the pockets. The uniform was well worn. She felt like she'd stepped into the days of WW II. Both the pockets were ripped but there was a small book in one. Betty felt guilty but reached in and pulled out a small bible. Its leather cover was turned and bent and the pages had creases in them as if they had been held tightly and folded in half to fit inside the pocket. Some verses had been underlined and there was a name inside the front cover, with a date. A yellowed letter fell onto the floor when she went to put the bible back into the pocket.

Now I am intruding, she thought. *But this place is now ours now so I'm going to read it anyway!*

Dear Gloria,

If you're reading this letter, it means I won't be coming home. I don't have any regrets fighting for my country. Words cannot express my enduring love for you, and I'll keep you safe in my heart forever—no matter where you are.

May looking back at all our wonderful memories bring comfort to you now and forever.

Until we meet again,
Your true love,
Michael

Tears were slowly leaking from Betty's eyes. Now she knew the story of the wedding gown and the uniform. Two people who loved each other and planned to live the rest of their lives together with hope and joy had worn them.

***

Chapter 36
Runaways

The two friends had finally decided to start their journey. They'd been planning to run away and now they were ready. Backpacks were full, snacks were made, and all the necessities were packed.

Sophia had $20.00 in her pocket. She'd been thinking about this adventure ever since she and Betty started to talk and getting excited about plans for their trip. Sophia would meet Betty at the ferry depot to catch a ship to Vancouver. She couldn't sleep that night, so she was up early. Grabbing her backpack, she tiptoed out the front door before her mom and dad woke up.

The ferry terminal was within walking distance of her house. It was still dark as she headed off down the road. The branches of some huge willow trees were draping down almost to the level of the sidewalks. Sophia made herself walk a lot faster. The darkness was like a black cloak silencing her steps.

Turning the corner, she saw Betty standing at the terminal and waved to her. Betty was grinning as Sophia approached. She could see that Betty was getting excited, so she ran the rest of the way to meet her. The ferry was coming in, and Betty had already bought tickets.

When the ferry docked, they scurried down the steps and found a seat with an ocean view. Betty had called her father, who lived in White Rock. He said he'd pick them up, thinking they were coming for a short visit. He would welcome them warmly. Betty told Sophia she was sad her mom and dad weren't living together anymore. She said she had a stepmom she didn't like.

The girls bought cokes at the deli, anticipating a long ride.

When the ferry arrived in Vancouver, they ran down the gangplank to meet Betty's dad, who was already waiting in the terminal. Betty ran over to hug him and introduce him to Sophia. Then they climbed into her dad's car and headed for White Rock.

When they got there, Betty's dad made the girls hot dogs and hamburgers. Judy was so full after the meal that she was ready for bed. Betty asked her dad if he'd drive them to a mall in the morning after breakfast. He said he would. After Betty's father dropped them off at the mall, he said goodbye. Beth and Judy had plans to run away to California. There, they thought they'd find beaches, warm weather and freedom—with no one telling them what they should or shouldn't do with their lives. It'd be the cool life of a hippie with no responsibilities.

Soon after they started hitchhiking, a van pulled over, and the two men inside said they'd take them over the border. They told them to hide in the back of the vehicle and drove to a friend's house. The friend fed them and talked to them for a while until the girls felt tired. Then, they pitched their tent in the backyard. Feeling safe, they fell asleep.

The next day, they ate breakfast and thanked the men and their friend for everything. They started to hitchhike again, hoping to reach California in a couple of days. A station wagon with a man in it pulled over, and the driver smiled and said, "Where are you two headed?"

"We're going to California," replied Betty.

"Come on then, hop in—that's where I'm going too."

Once the girls got comfortable, the man never stopped talking. They noticed many cute puppies in the back of the station wagon, inside boxes. All of a sudden, the man turned onto a gravel road.

Betty and Sophia looked at each other wide-eyed, not knowing what to expect. Eventually, he turned down another dirt road that led to a farmyard. He got out of the car. "Stay here," he said, "I'll be back in a minute."

Betty and Sophia looked at each other, waiting for the other one to make a decision. Just as suddenly, the car door opened, and the man hopped in. As soon as they got back to the highway, they asked the man to stop and got out of his car, thanking him for the ride.

Betty suggested to Sophia, "We'll get picked up faster if we put our bathing suits on." By this time, Sophia was ready to go home.

They walked for a while along the highway, listening to horns honking as they watched many vehicles race past them. Finally, an elderly couple pulled over on their way to Santa Barbara. The woman scolded them and demanded that they put their clothes back on. Then, the couple took the girls to a police station, and the staff sergeant called their parents, knowing how worried their mothers would be. Sophia's mom and dad borrowed money from a friend to take the bus to Santa Barbara.

Sophia was eager for her mom and dad to arrive, even though she didn't know what to expect for punishments. Betty said she wasn't ready to go home. Sophia looked at her and said, "Don't you care about how your parents will be worried for our safety?" Betty shrugged her shoulders.

When the bus pulled up and her mom and dad got off, Sophia ran up to them with tears in her eyes and said, "I'm so sorry."

Her mom held her in her arms.

Her dad said, "It's time to come home now."

Betty looked at them and said, "I'm not going back."

Sophia's mother gave Betty a stern look. "You'd better be on the bus by the time I come back with tickets," she stated emphatically.

Betty looked at Sophia's mom and felt very scared. Then she ran to get on the bus.

To this day, the girls still can't believe they took what could have turned out to be a very dangerous journey.

***

Chapter 37
Living a Sustainable Life

Most people who live off the grid have a pioneer spirit and choose to live that way. It is not what you imagine until you have experienced it. Living off the grid can be extremely risky. They strive toward a calmer, self-sustaining lifestyle. Most of these people prefer to keep it simple, that being their reason for living off the grid.

Your health is an important factor.   If medication is long-term, then arrangements need to be organized with a doctor and pharmacist.

There are no connections to public utilities, sewers, water, and electrical lines. So, where do you get all these amenities?
You do not get them; you invent them.!

Your work will be cut out for you, requiring a lot of physical labour to get settled. People who choose to live off the grid usually have basic skills in fishing, hunting, and gardening.
Also, they have a good knowledge of first aid.

There are pros and cons to living off the grid.
- You save money!
- It's great for the environment!
- Ways of making money are having farm markets, roadside vegetable stands, and private customers to sell produce and deliver.
- Grow a garden for neighbours in the off-the-grid community to come and "pick and pay system."
- Learn how to preserve for the harshest winters. If you are going to work with animals, you need to learn and study them inside and out. Raise chickens, ducks, sheep, and goats for food and other various uses.

- Many people use their skills making pottery, cheese, canning homegrown products, and selling them.
- It all depends on how far off the grid; you could be a trail guide and have retreats. Some people keep their jobs, requiring Wi-Fi.
- Some people use generators, and others prefer to use candles and lamps if necessary.
- A disposal for sewage waste, a septic spot is required, and an outhouse can be built, unless you prefer to have an indoor bathroom and have some plumbing knowledge.
- Drinking water is boiled or purchased when buying supplies, depending on the location and how far off the grid they may be.
- Most people do quite a lot of research and testing before they decide to put their ideas to work, even though sometimes it may be trial and error!
- When choosing a location to live off the grid, water is an important resource. Ponds, creeks, lakes, or rivers.
- Solar energy is an alternative for people who plan to stay for a long stretch of time.
- To store food takes a lot of thought and time, to keep cold and from spoilage.
- A wood stove is used for cooking and heating the home.

Living off the grid is rewarding to some people; while there are others that do not find it their bag of tricks. They feel that having no instant amenities is not the way to live.

**

ABOUT THE AUTHOR

Penny E. Ross enjoys writing and telling stories about her childhood on the Canadian prairies and her adult life on Vancouver Island and in Northern Alberta.

Her love for writing and art began in elementary school when she discovered short stories, poetry, and drawing. As she grew up, Penny explored painting, photography, and many other creative expressions. ***Once Upon a Time…Along My Way*** is Penny's first collection of short stories, and she is working on a second book. Penny has also illustrated two children's books written by RP Mickelson: ***One Day with Big and Little Ellie*** and **A Children's Book of Stories**.

www.ingramcontent.com/pod-product-compliance
Lightning Source LLC
Chambersburg PA
CBHW031112260626
47172CB00001B/332